"You don't understand. I don't want Kit."

I stopped, struck by an embarrassing new thought. I said bitterly, "You're sorry for me. That's why you invited me to Greece in the first pl~~~~

There w~ very quie~ think tha~ here, Ann~

I caught m~ ~~~~ a sob. "What other reason is there?" I asked wildly.

"This," he said harshly, and suddenly his mouth came down on mine in a long, hard, thrilling kiss that seemed to last forever.

There was a movement at the door. Ran swore softly as he released me and turned. A dark, slender woman came running across the room to him, arms outstretched. "Ran, oh, Ran." It was my rival, Venetia....

Many of these titles are available at your local bookseller.

For a free catalogue listing all available Harlequin Romances, send your name and address to:

HARLEQUIN READER SERVICE,
M.P.O. Box 707, Niagara Falls, N.Y. 14302
Canadian address: Stratford, Ontario, Canada N5A 6W2

Heart of the Scorpion

by

JANICE GRAY

Harlequin Books

TORONTO·LONDON·NEW YORK·AMSTERDAM
SYDNEY·HAMBURG·PARIS·STOCKHOLM

Original hardcover edition published 1979
by Mills & Boon Limited

ISBN 0-373-02294-8

Harlequin edition published in November 1979

Printed in U S A.

CHAPTER ONE

NOTHING had changed. As my father's somewhat battered shooting brake turned into the narrow, winding lane that led past stately Armitage Hall towards our own more homely farmhouse my mind registered the fact with an almost surprised pleasure. Whenever I came home from university—and I had been there almost three years now—I experienced a momentary qualm lest everything should not be exactly as I remembered it, but each time my first glimpse of Mother standing in the doorway, her face wreathed in a welcoming smile, was enough to reassure me. Mother didn't like changes any more than I did.

Today, on this grey, rather bleak March afternoon our house, as always, seemed warm and welcoming, with a huge log fire blazing in the sitting room, daffodils gleaming brightly in bowls and vases and our big, red-tiled kitchen full of the delicious smell of newly baked bread. Unlike me, Mother was domesticated: she really enjoyed cooking and running a home. I thought perhaps I might enjoy it too, one day, but not yet.

'Darling, it's lovely to have you home again!' Mother said, hugging me. And then, looking at me in the way that mothers often do look at their offspring after a period of absence, 'But you're much too pale, Annabel, and you've got some horrid dark circles be-

neath your eyes!' She shook her head. 'Too many
end-of-term parties, I suppose?'

I, pretended to look affronted. 'I've been working
really hard: burning the midnight oil, in fact. Yes,
truly!' as Mother raised an incredulous eyebrow. 'As
I shall be taking my Finals next term I thought it
would be simply silly not to.'

'My sensible daughter.' Mother sounded surprised
but approving. 'You've grown up a lot in the last
eighteen months or so, Annabel.'

'Well, so I should hope!' I retorted, laughing. 'I'm
nearly twenty-one, remember.'

Mother sighed. 'I do remember. It seems only yesterday, though, that I was having to deal with grazed
knees and lost hair-ribbons and torn jeans and black
eyes——'

I pulled a face at her. 'I only ever had one black
eye, Mother dear, and that was entirely thanks to
Kit's erratic bowling!'

I spoke without rancour, for Kit Armitage, the
bowler I had just referred to, had been my best friend
for as long as I could remember. There was, however,
no sign of a reminiscent smile on Mother's face.

'You may have had only one black eye, but you
broke a leg when you and Kit were out birds'-nesting
together and you cracked a couple of ribs when——'

'Stop!' I protested, laughing. 'You make me wonder how on earth I managed to survive at all!'

'You probably wouldn't have if Kit hadn't been
sent away to boarding school,' Mother said a little
tartly. 'You and he did nearly both drown once, do
you remember? It was Ran who saved you, bless his
heart.'

'He was beastly to us,' I said ungratefully, scowling at the long-ago memory. 'He boxed Kit's ears and I think he would have quite liked to box mine, too.'

'He had every right to be angry. You'd both been warned that the ice on the pond wasn't thick enough for skating,' Mother retorted. 'I hate to think what might have happened if Ran hadn't acted with such presence of mind.'

She turned away to make a pot of tea and I sat down at the kitchen table, watching her with my chin cupped in my hands. Ran and Kit. Those names were as familiar to me as if they had belonged to my brothers. Ran Armitage was several years older than me and had always held himself a little aloof, but Kit and I were almost the same age. As children we'd been inseparable and I'd been really miserable when Kit had had to go away to boarding school. He'd hated it, too. He wasn't brainy, like Ran, who at the age of twenty-eight was a Professor of Astro-Physics and to my mind, at least, almost scarifyingly clever.

'I thought you said in one of your letters that you had a chance to go to Italy this Easter,' Mother said, putting a large fruit cake on the table. 'What went wrong—couldn't you afford it? Your father and I might have been able to help——'

I shook my head. 'No, it wasn't that. It was going to be a ridiculously cheap holiday—a special cut-price thing for students. I'd practically made up my mind to go, actually, but then I had a letter from Kit. He said he'd definitely be coming home for Easter and that he hoped we'd be able to see something of each other.'

'So you changed your mind? Just on the strength

of Kit's letter?' Mother's face was subtly unreadable.

I flushed but answered her defiantly. 'You know I'd rather be with Kit than with almost anyone else. And I haven't seen him for ages—almost a year. It was last May when he went to Athens, wasn't it, to stay with his mother's family?'

Mother nodded. 'Yes. I was beginning to think that perhaps he'd made up his mind to stay there permanently. What exactly is he doing, Annabel? I know there was some talk of his going into his uncle's firm——'

'That fell through,' I told her. 'Shipping was too dull for Kit. I think just lately he's been dabbling in antiques.'

Mother sighed. 'I wish he'd gone to university, the way Ran wanted.'

I stiffened. 'Why should he always have to do what Ran wants? Just because he's his elder brother——'

'You've always taken Kit's side, Annabel.' Mother's smile was a little wry. 'You've never really got on well with Ran, have you?'

I didn't answer, but I felt my cheeks grow warm. Even Mother, discerning woman though she was, had never guessed at my most closely guarded secret, that although it was Kit who was my best friend I'd been crazily in love with Ran Armitage ever since I was about twelve years old. He didn't know that either, of course. Desperately afraid of being teased and mocked at—for what, after all, is more ludicrous than a bad case of calf-love?—I'd gone to extremes to make everyone, including Ran himself, think that I didn't particularly like him. It had seemed to me to be better for him to regard me as a rather bothersome child instead of an object of ridicule or pity.

I must have been a good actress, for no one had ever questioned my apparent dislike of Ran any more than they had questioned my genuine affection for Kit. They were so different, those two. Kit was a cheerful, happy-go-lucky extrovert, whereas Ran, with his reserve, his wry humour, his mockery and his unexpectedness, was a far more complex character altogether. Perhaps it wasn't surprising that they didn't understand each other—that they always seemed to be at loggerheads.

I sighed. The last time I'd seen Ran was over two years ago, when his father and mother, tragic victims of a motorway pile-up, had been buried in the church-yard of our little fifteenth-century village church. After the funeral Ran and Kit, for once united in their grief, had come to our house for lunch and I could remember passionately hoping that their new-found amity would last. It hadn't, of course. Ran had been disappointed by his brother's refusal to go to univer-sity, and he hadn't been too pleased when Kit had de-cided to remove himself to Greece, either. I thought he had been unfair over that. Ran's and Kit's mother had been Greek and both boys had been brought up to think of Greece as their second home.

Mother's voice interrupted my thoughts. 'When exactly is Kit coming home?'

'He should be at the Hall now,' I said, heaping two large teaspoonfuls of sugar into my tea. 'He told me in his last letter that he was going to try and book his flight for the fifteenth.'

Mother frowned. 'Ran came back from the States

last month. I met him in the village yesterday and he didn't say anything about Kit being at home. Mind you, I only spoke to him for a second——'

'I expect he didn't think it was worth mentioning.' Even to my own ears my voice sounded a little acid. 'I think perhaps I'll give the Hall a ring——'

Mother looked at me. 'Don't you think it would be rather more—well, dignified—to wait a little, Annabel? You've only just this moment arrived.'

'Oh, Mother!' I couldn't help laughing. 'When have Kit and I ever worried about dignity?'

'Never. But, as you've just pointed out, you are nearly twenty-one now. Perhaps it's time you should start worrying,' Mother said a little crisply.

I stared at her and perhaps my expression was hurt and puzzled, for she spoke quickly.

'Darling, it won't be the end of the world if you don't see or speak to Kit until tomorrow,' she said gently. 'Let your father and me have you to ourselves for tonight, at least.'

Something about her voice—a hint of wistfulness —alerted me to trouble. 'What's wrong?' I demanded.

Mother sighed. 'It's your father's Aunt Isobel. She's not been very well just lately and she wants to see us. We've arranged to go at the end of next week. You can come with us, too, of course, if you want to——'

I grimaced and shook my head. I didn't much care for Aunt Isobel and I hated her big, gloomy house in Scotland where there was nothing to do and no one of my own age group to talk to. Besides, there was Kit. If I spent half of my vacation north of the Border I might just as well have gone to Italy!

I said, 'I think I'll stay here. Kit and I can pool resources.'

Mother laughed. 'Poor Kit if he relies on you to feed him adequately! How many tins of baked beans did I find in your cupboard the last time I came to visit you? Your staple diet, you informed me——'

I grinned. 'Sue and Philippa and I are hard-up students, Mother dear. If we want to buy books and records and see something of the world during our vacations we can't afford fancy cooking!'

'Well, there's nothing fancy about steak and kidney pudding, and that's what I'm giving you for dinner tonight,' Mother said, and I flung my arms around her neck.

'Angel mother! You know how I adore steak and kidney pudding! Thank goodness I don't need to hold up my hands in horror and say "Oh, but I'm slimming?"'

'No,' Mother said, giving me a judicial look. 'You're really quite an attractive shape, Annabel. You were a bit on the skinny side a couple of years ago, but you've filled out now quite nicely.'

'Let's hope Kit thinks so, too,' I said naughtily, and then chuckled as I saw Mother lift an eyebrow.

'You needn't look at me like that! You know quite well that I'm only joking. Kit looks upon me as a sister!' I assured her.

'Hm. I'm not so sure that he will now. Athens will have sophisticated him a bit, and you aren't exactly the girl he used to play rounders and cricket with, you know,' Mother said drily.

I went pink. Did Mother perhaps wonder if I was secretly hoping that one day my friendship with Kit

would blossom into something else? Nearly everyone in the village seemed to think that eventually I'd
end up as Mrs Kit Armitage—at any rate just recently
I'd had a lot of winks and nudges whenever his name
was mentioned. No one had any way of knowing that
I was quite, quite, sure that I could never think of
Kit as anything but a very good friend . . . that it was
his elder brother's dark, handsome face which still
haunted my dreams and made it impossible for me to
think of any other man in a romantic context.

I was, however, human enough to want Kit to find
me attractive. The next morning, after I had decided
to set out immediately after breakfast to visit the
Hall, I looked into the mirror and couldn't help feeling pretty well satisfied with what I saw. Kit had
probably had a surfeit of dark-haired, dark-eyed
Grecian beauties: he might find my golden hair and
very blue eyes a refreshing change!

I smiled at the thought and then scowled at the
dimples which immediately appeared in my cheeks.
How I hated those wretched dimples! I'd been told
that they were fascinating, but I longed to get rid of
them. It was Ran who once, a long time ago, had
sarcastically remarked that my curls and dimples and
my adoration of Kit reminded him of Violet Elizabeth
in Richmal Crompton's 'William' books. It was an in-
sult for which I had never really forgiven him, even
now.

Mother had suggested that I ought to phone Kit before visiting the Hall, but I had turned the suggestion
down. I wanted to surprise him. That's why, instead
of walking down the long, winding drive that led to

the front door of the Hall, I decided to make a detour through the rose garden.

It was a heavenly day, with the sun pouring down from a cloudless sky and touching the yellow lichen on the tiled roof of the deep-gabled, stately old house, making it almost golden. The flower borders were full of daffodils, the yellow trumpets making a glorious splash of colour against the dark hedges, and I found myself thinking that old Dick Barlow, who had been head gardener at the Hall ever since I could remember, was still doing a marvellous job.

There was somebody in the rose garden. His back was towards me and just for a moment I thought that it was Kit. Then my heart missed a beat and my stomach twisted with an old familiar feeling. That dark hair, curling in an almost sculptured fashion, didn't belong to Kit. It wasn't Kit who was standing there. It was Ran.

He hadn't changed a bit. He was just as I remembered him, the most handsome man I had ever known —handsome not in the smooth matinee idol style but with a dark, hard leanness that was even more devastating. He was casually dressed in light slacks and a burnt orange shirt which accentuated his darkness— the darkness that he had inherited from his beautiful Greek mother. Kit was very fair, like his father ... like me.

Ran was staring at me. I saw the puzzled expression on his face and spoke breathlessly. 'Hullo. Don't you remember me?'

For a moment he didn't speak, then a look of startled recognition crept into his eyes and he laughed.

'Yes, of course. It's the long hair that momentarily threw me, plus—er—one or two other things. It's Violet Elizabeth, isn't it?'

I went scarlet. I said furiously, 'I suppose you think that's funny! Well, I'm afraid I *don't*! I'm not a child any longer——'

I stopped, choking. This wasn't how I'd visualised my first meeting with Ran for two years. I'd meant to be a little distant, a little aloof ... I'd meant to show him how worldly and sophisticated I'd become. I certainly hadn't expected him to start provoking me into wanting to make the kind of adolescent wise-cracks that had always bounced straight off him, anyway.

I would have turned on my heel and marched away, but Ran put out his hand and caught hold of my arm. I hadn't bothered with a coat and his fingers were warm against my bare skin.

'I'm sorry! Don't be mad at me, Annabel. I agree, it wasn't at all funny. You're not a little girl any more and I've absolutely no right to tease you. Please for-give me.'

Somewhat mollified, I said stiffly, 'Violet Elizabeth never was a very nice name to call me, even when I was a little girl.'

Ran's lips quirked. 'You never told me you ob-jected.'

'Kit said if I did it would probably make you do it all the more.' I spoke defensively.

The laughter died out of Ran's eyes. 'Yes, I suppose Kit probably would have thought along those lines.' He drew a long breath. 'Anyway, what do you want?'

'To see Kit, of course,' I said coolly.

Ran stared at me. 'Kit?'

There was so much surprise in his voice that sudden alarm seized me. 'He—he is here, isn't he?'

'Kit?' Ran repeated his brother's name slowly. 'You expected to find *Kit* here?'

I caught my breath. 'Yes. Yes, of course I did! He wrote to me from Athens, ages ago, to tell me that he was coming home for Easter. He even told me which day he was going to try and book his flight. He should have arrived on Tuesday!'

There was a moment's silence. The sun had momentarily gone behind a cloud and the day had lost its brightness. Ran's face was set in an expression I was unable to read, but when he spoke his voice was quiet and dispassionate.

'Well, I'm sorry. I'm afraid he must have changed his mind, since I'm the only member of the Armitage family in residence.'

I was bewildered. 'But—but he *can't* have changed his mind! He would have written to tell me!' Then as Ran made no answer, 'When did *you* last hear from him?'

A faint smile twisted Ran's lips. 'I really can't remember. Kit and I don't exactly bombard each other with correspondence, you know, Annabel.'

'No, of course not, but——' I stopped, too much shaken off balance to think clearly. Perhaps Kit had been unavoidably delayed. Perhaps he'd arrive today or tomorrow or even the next day.

Ran was watching my face. 'Why don't you come into the house and have a cup of coffee? Then you can tell me exactly what Kit said in his letter and perhaps we can take it from there,' he suggested.

Something inside me warned me that I should refuse his invitation, but despite the faint prickle of nervous excitement along my skin, my quickened heartbeat, I did nothing of the sort. Instead I nodded.

'All right. Thank you.'

A flight of shallow stone steps at one end of the rose garden led to french windows which opened into a cool, dark-panelled library. It was a beautiful room, but since Ran's visits to the Hall were infrequent it had a bare, unlived-in look which made me give a slight shiver.

'Are you cold?' Ran turned to me quickly. 'That dress is a bit on the thin side, isn't it? Why on earth didn't you wear something warmer?'

I didn't answer, but perhaps my expression gave me away, for Ran suddenly grinned.

'Vanity, thy name is woman. Did you hope to dazzle Kit? It's certainly a very becoming garment, though just at the moment I have to admit that the goose-pimples do rather detract from the overall effect.'

I flushed. 'Didn't you say something about a cup of coffee?' I asked pointedly.

'I did. Give me five minutes.' Still grinning, Ran disappeared and I sat down in a big, velvet-covered armchair. There was a photograph of Kit on the bureau beside me and I picked it up and studied it intently. It was a good likeness. His lips were smiling and his eyes full of sparkling mockery that denied the seriousness of life. Kit played at everything—even, I had no doubt, at falling in love.

'Here you are.' Ran's voice behind me made me

jump. 'Put this on. At least it will stop you from freezing to death.'

He was holding out a thick navy-blue sweater. I hesitated and Ran's mouth went down at one corner.

'You surely don't care what impression you make on me?'

Wordlessly I snatched the sweater and put it on. It was only then that—belatedly—I remembered my manners. 'Thank you.'

'Don't mention it. Now for that coffee,' Ran said cheerfully.

I hesitated again. 'Can I help?'

'You can come and talk to me if you like. I've been thinking. How long ago did Kit write to you? And are you quite sure he definitely said that he was booking a flight for the fifteenth?'

'Quite sure. I—I don't understand it, Ran. Kit knew I was turning down the chance of a fortnight in Italy just—just to see him. He wouldn't let me down! I—I know he wouldn't!'

There was a little silence. Then very quietly Ran said, 'Don't you think it's about time you outgrew that rather dangerous idea you've always had that Kit can do no wrong, Annabel? He's a human being, you know, and he has faults and frailties just like everyone else.'

'I might have known you'd say something like that.' In spite of myself my voice shook. Obviously Ran was amongst those who thought that I was head over heels in love with Kit. Well, what difference did it make if he did? As long as he never suspected the way I really felt, about him. . . .

Ran looked at me. 'You think I'm too hard on Kit, don't you? You always have.'

'It isn't really any of my business.' I spoke stiffly. 'Look, shall we get on with making that coffee? I really could do with a cup.'

'So could I.' Ran's voice was grim and when I stole a glance at him I saw that he was frowning. Without saying any more he led the way into the kitchen, where I found two cups and saucers and put them on a tray while Ran filled the electric kettle and switched it on. Kit, I thought suddenly, would have left all that to me, but Ran was as neat-handed as a sailor for all his size.

'I'm afraid it'll have to be instant coffee. Do you mind?' he asked.

I laughed. 'I never drink anything else but instant coffee when I'm at college. Probably we won't even be able to afford that next term!'

Ran looked as though he was searching his memory. 'You're reading modern languages, aren't you? What are going to do when you leave?'

I shrugged. 'I don't really know yet. I may go abroad or I may decide to stay here and teach for a year or two.'

'What then? Every girl's dream—marriage and domesticity?' Ran enquired mockingly.

I struggled to keep my temper. 'You're way behind the times. That *isn't* every girl's dream these days, and it certainly isn't mine.'

Ran's eyes held a disturbing gleam. 'That's fighting talk from a girl who was content to spend her entire childhood and adolescence tagging along behind my young brother! Does Kit know you've become a fully paid up member of the Women's Lib movement?'

I dropped a spoon. 'I'm not a Women's Libber!' I said angrily. 'All I said was that I didn't think that marriage was necessarily the be-all and end-all of everything.'

'Quite right,' Ran agreed.

I looked at him and even though I was so annoyed with him I couldn't help realising anew how attractive he was ... how good the lines of his back and shoulder under the thin cotton of his shirt. I couldn't help wondering, too, how many other women found him as attractive as I did. He'd always had lots of girl-friends, though as far as I could remember there was only one he'd ever been really interested in. Her name had been Venetia and she'd been a model ... a tall, willowy brunette with raven-black hair, huge dark eyes and the kind of complexion that made you think of porcelain. She and Ran had been constant companions for the whole of one summer and everyone had been certain that wedding bells were in the air. Something must have gone very wrong, though, because suddenly Venetia had stopped coming to the Hall and a few months later Kit had told me that she had decided to marry someone else ... Paul Forrest, a very well-known and successful television reporter who also happened to be one of Ran's best friends. He was a widower; his first wife, Louise, had died giving birth to a baby girl who'd become Ran's goddaughter.

Oddly enough, in view of the circumstances, Paul's and Venetia's marriage had not meant the end of their friendship with Ran, and that had surprised a lot of people, including Kit. He seemed to be sure that although Ran managed to hide the fact behind an elaborate smoke-screen, he was still desperately in love with Venetia and found it very hard to accept that she was now another man's wife. I, of course, had no way of knowing if that were true or not. I only knew that I wanted Ran to be happy, even if I myself could never have a part in that happiness.

'A penny for your thoughts.' Ran's voice was soft, his brows lifted enquiringly.

I blushed. 'The kettle's boiling.'

'So it is.' Ran switched it off and unplugged it. We made the coffee, and then carried our cups out on to the terrace. It was warmer outside in the sun than it was in the house.

'It seems so odd without Kit.' I spoke almost without thinking and I saw Ran's thick brows draw together in a frown. He said nothing, however, and after a moment or two I swallowed hard.

'I've said it before, but I'll say it again. I don't believe Kit would change his mind about coming home without—without letting me know, Ran. Perhaps—perhaps he's been taken ill. Or maybe he's had an accident——' In spite of myself my voice trembled.

Ran looked at me. 'Well, if it was anything serious surely you or I would have heard about it by now. These aren't exactly the Dark Ages, you know, Annabel. There's nothing very badly wrong with our modern systems of communications!'

There was a hint of exasperation in his voice and I bent my head so that my long fair hair fell over my face, hiding my expression.

After a moment Ran spoke again. 'You're still very fond of Kit, aren't you?' he asked, and this time, because his voice was kinder, I answered him.

'Yes.'

'Does he write to you often?'

I shook my head. 'No. He—he's busy, you see——'

'Busy?'

'He's helping a friend who runs an antique shop in Athens.'

Ran looked sceptical. 'Really? I'd have thought that what Kit knows about antiques wouldn't cover the back of a postage stamp!'

'Why do you always have to belittle him?' I asked indignantly. 'Just because he's not as brainy as you are——'

'There's nothing wrong with Kit's brains. He's just too lazy to use them, that's all,' Ran said shortly, and I glared at him.

'He isn't lazy! You've no right to say that!'

Ran's face wore an expression of sardonic amusement. 'There you go again. My hero, right or wrong!' he said caustically.

I gritted my teeth. I didn't say anything, though, and after a moment or two I saw that Ran was smiling.

'You have a very expressive face, Annabel. Why don't you just go right ahead and tell me exactly what you think of me?' he suggested.

I drew a deep breath. 'Ran——'

'It's all right. I won't hold the fact that you dislike me against you.' Ran spoke as lightly as before, but again there was that disturbing gleam in his dark eyes.

'I don't——' I stopped, afraid of being betrayed into an indiscretion. I couldn't bear Ran to know how

I really felt about him. Not ever.

'I don't know you all that well.' I spoke lamely and Ran laughed.

'You've known me all your life! Don't prevaricate, Annabel,' he said, wilfully misunderstanding me. And then, as I flushed, 'Of course, I have been away rather a lot just lately.'

'Yes, you have.' Thankfully seizing the chance to change the subject, I added politely, 'Do you like your work?'

'Very much, thank you. I wouldn't do it if I didn't.'

I bit my lip. 'You must tell me about it some time. Astronomy ... it's a very interesting subject.'

Ran's lips twitched. 'Sure you're not thinking of astrology?'

I knew he was teasing me and I was indignant. 'Of course not! Though astrology is interesting, too.' I looked at him defiantly. 'I always read my horoscope. I suppose you disapprove?'

'Of something that apparently gives you pleasure? Why on earth should I?'

Ran answered me so calmly that I knew he wasn't going to let himself be drawn into an argument which would give me an excuse to prolong my visit. Sighing inwardly, I finished my coffee and set the cup down.

'I've got to go. I told Mother I'd be back by twelve and it's nearly that now.'

Ran frowned. 'Have you decided what you're going to do about Kit?'

'Nothing. I still think he'll turn up in the next two or three days.'

'How nice to have such touching faith in someone.' Ran spoke sardonically. 'Take my advice, Annabel. Forget about Kit. Enjoy your holiday. Have fun——'

'Ran,' I clenched my hands, 'I can't forget Kit, even if you can. And I can't help worrying about him, either——'

'Then you're very foolish. Worrying about Kit is a singularly pointless occupation. That's something I discovered a long time ago,' Ran said drily. 'You're probably right. He'll turn up—eventually, with or without a valid excuse for letting you down.'

I was so angry with him that I walked away without even saying goodbye. Unfortunately, my exit from the terrace was ruined by the fact that I was still wearing Ran's sweater and I had to stop and take it off. I suppose I could have worn it all the way home and returned it to Ran later on, but I decided to resist the temptation. I didn't think it would be wise to make another visit to Armitage Hall, not while Kit wasn't there.

A day or two later a card came bearing Kit's almost illegible scrawl. The message, brief though it was, dashed all my hopes.

'Sorry I can't manage to get home for a few days after all. Will explain later. At present am staying with friends in Salonika but will let you know when I return to Athens. Love, Kit.'

I wasn't angry with him—however badly he behaved, only Ran ever seemed to get angry with Kit, and anyway, it wasn't his fault that his message had been delayed—but I *was* puzzled and disappointed. And I hated to think that Ran had been proved right

... that there hadn't been any need to worry. Obviously something rather more attractive than a holiday in England had cropped up for Kit and so at the last moment he'd changed his plans. It was just like him. Reliability had never been one of his strongest points—except he'd never ever let *me* down before!

Mother—sweet Mother—sympathised with my disappointment but couldn't understand why I was so upset when I learned that not only had she passed the gist of Kit's message on to Ran but that she had also invited him to dinner on Sunday evening. I tried to explain that I knew Ran wouldn't be sympathetic —that in fact he was probably laughing at me up his sleeve—but she simply said that I was being ridiculous.

'Poor Ran! Why you always insist on regarding him as an ogre I'll never know,' she said with such heat that for the moment I was silenced.

When Sunday evening came I hinted that I'd be a lot happier with a tray in my room, but Mother wouldn't hear of it. I was so reluctant to face Ran, though, that I was still dressing when I saw him coming towards the house. He looked, I thought with a stab of pain, even more handsome in his well-cut suit than he had looked in his colourful shirt, though it wasn't only his blazing good looks that I'd fallen in love with. Everything about him gave me secret satisfaction—the way he walked and talked, the way he smiled, his deep voice and mouth that could be either stern or gentle. He was so tall, too ... why had I never realised before how tall he was? He must top his younger brother by at least a couple of inches.

I sighed as I zipped up my dress. It was a new one

and made me look so much older and more sophisticated that when I looked in my mirror even I could see little resemblance between the girl whose reflected face stared back at me and the denim-clad tomboy of a year or two ago. Surely even Ran must realise, tonight, that I was no longer a child?

Overcoming my reluctance, I went downstairs, waiting until Ran had been welcomed inside and the chink of glasses told me that Father was serving drinks. I could hear, as I approached the door, the murmur of voices, and though I didn't really mean to eavesdrop I caught one of Father's little speeches quite distinctly.

'Annabel has always had a blind spot where Kit is concerned,' I heard him say. 'She's utterly devoted to him and always has been, as you very well know. I could wring his neck for letting her down over this holiday. She's done nothing but mope ever since his card came.'

I didn't wait to hear what Ran would answer. My cheeks burning, I opened the door and walked in. I even managed to return Ran's lazy smile, though I could have done without my father's appreciative whistle.

'Good heavens! I hadn't realised I had such a beautiful daughter!'

I felt the colour rise and wash through my cheeks as I caught Ran's eye. I only hoped that he didn't think that I'd spent a couple of hours prinking in front of a mirror, because I certainly hadn't. It just happened to be one of those very rare occasions when everything—my dress, my hair, my skin—looked absolutely perfect without any effort on my part whatsoever.

Dinner was delicious—Mother had excelled herself —but as far as I was concerned it could well have been sawdust. At any rate Ran seemed to enjoy it. He was very much at ease with my parents: I could see how much he liked them and how much they liked him.

'It's good to have you back with us again, Ran,' Mother said. 'I wish your work didn't take you away quite so often. I'd like to see you settle down at the Hall with a pretty young wife and raise a large family.'

Mother was nothing if not old-fashioned, I thought, but Ran only laughed.

'One small difficulty, Mrs Conway. First I have to find a girl brave enough to take me on.'

'That shouldn't be any problem,' said Mother, smiling.

Ran shook his head. 'I'm afraid it is. I don't seem to attract the really nice girls: they find my charms very easy to resist,' he said with mock pathos, and looked straight at me.

'Oh, I'm sure you're being much too modest, Ran,' I said with false sweetness, and to my annoyance I saw his lips twitch in amusement.

Mother took one look at our faces and smoothly changed the subject by asking Ran something about his future plans.

'My very wealthy and delightfully philanthropic Uncle Xenophon is lending me his yacht, so for a couple of weeks I intend to cruise around some of my favourite Greek islands,' Ran told us. 'With luck, I'll end up in Crete, where Uncle Xenophon has a holiday villa which he has also put at my disposal.'

Absentmindedly I helped myself to more potatoes than I really wanted. I'd heard quite a lot about Ran's and Kit's Uncle Xenophon over the years. He was a millionaire shipowner who seemed to enjoy spending his money on making other people happy, and since he was childless and Elena Armitage had been his only sister he had always been particularly generous to his two nephews.

My father gave a sigh of mock envy. 'That's the kind of relative to have! Lucky man. While Stella and I are shivering in misty Scotland we'll think of you basking in the sun, surrounded, no doubt, by a bevy of bikini-clad beauties——'

'Jack!' Mother looked at him reprovingly and Ran laughed.

'It won't be quite like that, I'm afraid. My travelling companion will be my small goddaughter.'

Mother raised her brows. 'You mean Tamsin?'

'Yes. Paul's and Venetia's *au pair* has unexpectedly given in her notice and it's put Venetia in rather a spot as she's due to fly to New York on a modelling assignment. She hasn't a hope of finding a replacement for Françoise in the time available and Paul can't help out—he's abroad, filming. So, taking my courage in both hands, I've volunteered to take Tamsin with me and look after her until Venetia is able to join us in Crete.'

There was a small silence, during which I was attacked by that most unattractive of sins—envy. I'd never been to any of the Greek Islands, but I'd always wanted to. Just the thought of them—beautiful, romantic, alluringly different—acted on me like an enchanter's wand. Lucky Tamsin! I shut my eyes, conjuring up a vision of island-studded seas ... long, hot, sun-soaked days ... velvety, star-spangled nights. A holiday like that, with Ran, would be pure magic. ...

It was Mother who spoke first. 'That—that's very kind of you,' she said a little uncertainly. 'Are you sure you'll be able to manage, though? Tamsin can't be very old——'

'She's eight, and very sensible for her age,' Ran said. He paused, then added casually, 'I've seen quite a bit of her just lately, actually. As you probably know, Paul's work takes him all over the globe and Venetia has been finding it rather difficult to cope single-handed with Tamsin and her own career.'

Mother frowned. 'I thought someone told me that she'd decided to give up modelling——'

'She did, for a time. It's only quite recently that she's started working again,' Ran said briefly.

I kept my eyes on my plate. 'I don't believe he'll ever get over Venetia,' Kit had told me two years ago. 'There'll never be anyone else for him but her ... he'll never ever forget her.' I'd scoffed at him at the time, but now—well, now I wasn't so sure. He must still think a great deal of her, if he was willing to shoulder her responsibilities! Did Paul, Venetia's husband, know and approve? I wondered, and then was immediately angry with myself. It was none of my business: I had no right at all to speculate.

I suppose that it must have been halfway through the evening that Ran and I found ourselves alone together for a few minutes. I hastily searched my mind for some safe topic of conversation, but Ran fore-stalled me.

'I understand your parents are off to Scotland in a day or two. What are you proposing to do in their absence, Annabel?'

I shrugged. 'Nothing. Stay at home.' My eyes dared him to mention Kit, to say anything along the lines of, 'I told you so.'

He didn't. Instead he stood up and began, in a leisurely sort of way, to feel in his pockets for to-bacco. Then, quite calmly, he said, 'Would you like to come with Tamsin and me to Greece? The islands are beautiful: I believe you'd enjoy them.'

I stared at him. For a moment I thought he was joking, then I realised that he was perfectly serious.

'Wh-what did you say?'

Ran sighed, 'Annabel, I know you're not deaf. You heard me quite well. I asked you if you'd like to come to Greece with me.' Standing on the hearthrug, he looked down at me, searched my eyes. 'There are certain strings attached, of course. To be perfectly honest, I'd like someone to help me to amuse Tamsin, particularly while we're at sea.'

Resisting the temptation to pinch myself to see if I was dreaming, I found my voice at last. 'B-but why me? Surely if you advertised for help—applied to an agency——'

Ran shook his head. 'There really isn't time.' He paused, a wicked spark lighting his dark eyes. 'Any-way, you must have heard the old maxim! Better the devil you know——'

I stiffened. I wasn't dreaming after all. In my dreams Ran was always full of honey: it was only in real life that he was full of bees as well!

'You're not exactly flattering, are you?' I asked coldly.

Ran's lips quirked. 'I suppose not. But there's one thing I really can say in your favour, Annabel. There've been many times throughout our long acquaintance when I've longed to wring your neck, but at least you've never bored me!'

'Such magnanimity——'

Ran smiled at me in a way that I liked more than I would have believed possible. 'Don't be so prickly. Most women bore me very easily.' He struck a match. 'Naturally, if you did accept my proposition I'd be prepared to pay you an appropriate salary——'

I interrupted him quickly. 'You can forget about the salary, Ran. I must be honest. My experience of children is strictly limited——'

'So's mine. You needn't worry. Tamsin isn't a problem child, though she hasn't had too easy a time just lately. You're just what she needs—someone young and bright and cheerful——'

'Don't! You'll be calling me Pollyanna next.' I chose flippancy because I was afraid of any other response just then. 'That would be even worse than Violet Elizabeth!'

'Would it?'

'Much.' I spoke with conviction. 'In fact, I can't think of anything worse!'

'Come, come! Suppose I called you Cassandra, for instance? She was a gloomy creature, from all accounts——'

I laughed. 'Literally, the name means "snarer of men", so it's definitely inappropriate for me.'

Ran looked at me thoughtfully. 'I don't know so much. You're a very attractive young woman, you know.'

Despite the fact that his voice was completely dispassionate I felt the quick colour wash into my cheeks. 'Oh, but I'm not! At least, not when you compare me with someone like Venetia——'

I stopped, mentally cursing my stupidity, but once I'd started it seemed better to blunder on. 'She used to be incredibly lovely——'

Ran's face told me nothing. 'She still is. She hasn't changed at all.'

I swallowed. 'Is—is Tamsin pretty?'

Ran considered. 'Pretty? Yes, I suppose she is. At the moment she's very like her father.'

'I saw one of his television documentaries the other evening. I thought it was brilliant——'

'I'm sure it was. Paul's a brilliant man.'

I looked at him uncertainly, wondering if I had imagined the bleakness of his tone, a sudden hardness in the set of his mouth.

'Whereabouts is he filming now? He always seems to choose the most exotic, faraway places——'

'He's in Morocco.' Ran's answer was brief to the point of curtness and he gave me no chance to pursue the subject even if I'd wished to. 'Well, do you accept my proposition or not?' he asked.

Did he really think that there was a chance I'd refuse? I wondered. Did he really not know what piece of perfection he'd dropped into my lap? I took a deep breath and nodded.

'Yes, please. Yes, I do.'

I had no idea whether Ran was relieved by my

decision or not. 'Good. Then that's settled,' he said crisply.

'My parents——'

'Don't worry about them. Naturally I'll have to find out how they feel about the idea, but I don't somehow think they'll object. Your passport's okay, I suppose?'

'Yes.' I answered him a little shakily, still torn between conflicting emotions. 'When—when will we be going?'

'As soon as all the arrangements have been made. We'll fly to Athens and pick up Uncle Xenophon's yacht at Piraeus.' Ran hesitated. 'If you like you can try to contact Kit before we set sail——'

'He isn't in Athens at the moment. He's staying with friends in Salonika. Didn't Mother tell you?'

I tried to speak casually, but I don't think I quite succeeded, for I saw Ran frown.

'Did he tell you when he intends to return? No? Well then, you can phone his flat from the airport . . . see if he's back. You may be lucky,' he said, and then turned away to speak to my father, who had just come into the room with an armful of logs.

I knew that both he and my mother would probably be extremely surprised that I'd accepted Ran's offer, but I knew, too, that they wouldn't put any obstacles in my way. They liked Ran and they trusted us both. They had no way of knowing, thank goodness, how little I trusted myself.

CHAPTER TWO

'You must be Tamsin. I'm Annabel.' I smiled down at the small brown-haired, brown-eyed girl who stood staring solemnly at me while the thin, rather sallow-faced young woman who had just brought her to the departure lounge at London Airport launched herself at Ran and began talking at breakneck speed. Her English was good but her accent and gestures betrayed the fact that she was French. Venetia's *au pair*? I wondered. Probably, but if so where was Venetia herself?

Ran had told me, on our way to the airport, that he had arranged to meet Venetia and Tamsin at eleven o'clock. It was now twenty past and for the last ten minutes he had been glancing more and more anxiously at his watch. Punctuality, I had decided with a certain degree of smugness, was evidently not one of Venetia's outstanding virtues.

'We were caught in a traffic jam.' Tamsin, who wore a pretty cherry-coloured coat with a matching ribbon round the thick ponytail which she kept flicking from one shoulder to another, spoke gravely. 'I was awfully afraid we'd miss the plane. You were worried too, weren't you, Françoise?'

'A little worried, *chérie*,' Françoise agreed. She smiled apologetically at Ran. '*Mon dieu*—the traffic! Never have I seen so many buses all at one time!'

Ran looked across her at me and perhaps he saw puzzlement in my eyes, for he spoke quickly.

'This, as you'll have guessed, is Venetia's *au pair*, Françoise Deneuve. Venetia meant to bring Tamsin to the airport herself, but unfortunately at the last moment something else cropped up and she had to change her plans.'

'It was—how you say?—a mix-up!' Françoise said, spreading her hands and giving a little shrug of her slim shoulders, but though I smiled politely somewhere deep down I registered a tiny half-conscious alarm signal. What kind of a stepmother was Venetia that she couldn't put Tamsin first?

Our flight was being called. 'Have a good holiday, *ma petite*,' Françoise said to Tamsin, and she nodded and said, 'Thank you, Françoise' in a polite little voice. I wondered if she minded about parting with the French girl, but even if she did she showed no sign of tears. In fact, she seemed remarkably self-possessed.

I took a second, more careful look at her as we made our way to the plane and decided that although I didn't agree with Ran that she was pretty, there was nevertheless something very appealing about her small, heart-shaped face, and her big brown eyes were bright and sparkling. I could see her resemblance to her father: in spite of Tamsin's immaturity their features were very alike, straight and clear-cut.

Ran's deep voice cut across my thoughts. 'It's only a three-hour journey from here to Athens, Annabel. There'll be a hired car waiting for us at the airport, I hope, so that we can drive straight to Piraeus.'

'Great,' I said, and smiled at Tamsin. 'Have you ever flown before, Tamsin?'

'Lots of times,' said Tamsin, and Ran laughed.

'Oh, she's a seasoned traveller! You've been all over Europe with your father, haven't you, Tamsin?'

'Not since he married Venetia. We've got a proper home now, we didn't have before,' Tamsin explained as the three of us settled down in our row of high-backed seats and fastened our seat belts. 'It's only a flat, though. I wish we had a house in the country so we could keep lots of animals. What do you live in, Annabel—a flat or a proper house?'

'An old farmhouse. It's got a thatched roof and a big garden, with lots of fruit bushes and an orchard,' I told her.

'It sounds lovely! You live near Ran, don't you? Venetia told me that she thought she'd once met you at the Hall: you'd gone to tea with Kit.' Tamsin looked at me enquiringly. 'He's your boy-friend, isn't he? Are you going to marry him?'

I went scarlet. 'Tamsin——'

'Don't ask so many personal questions, my child.' Now that at last we were airborne Ran rose to throw Tamsin's cherry-coloured coat and my blue one expertly up into the rack. 'You're making poor Annabel blush.' His voice was pleasant, but at the same time it was edged with a mockery that I knew was intended specifically for me.

'Oh—sorry!' Tamsin looked dismayed. 'I thought —Venetia said——' She stopped, biting her lip.

I shot Ran an angry glance. 'It's all right, Tamsin. Kit isn't exactly my boy-friend, but I do like him very much indeed. I've known him a long time, you see.'

'I like him, too, but not half as much as I like Ran.' Tamsin spoke decidedly, then grinned up into his face.

'I have to like you best, don't I, because you're my godfather.'

'Is that the only reason?' Ran asked and Tamsin shook her head.

'You know it isn't. You're nice—nearly as nice as Daddy,' she said simply. 'Don't you think so, Annabel?'

'Very nice,' I agreed, and Ran gave me an amused look.

'Tongue well in cheek, I hope, Miss Conway?'

I was spared the need to answer by the arrival of a pretty blonde stewardess who asked us if we wanted anything to drink and who looked at Ran as though she liked what she saw. If I had been his girl-friend I might have been quite jealous of the way she smiled at him, I thought, and wondered, with a sense of disquiet, if any other woman would ever be able to take Venetia's place in his affections. Surely he wouldn't spend the rest of his life craving for something that was unattainable ... crying for the moon?

Another stewardess approached with a tray of papers and periodicals. Ran bought several, but none of them interested Tamsin. Instead she produced an Enid Blyton book which kept her quiet for the rest of the flight. Ran became absorbed in the *New Scientist* and I flicked over the pages of my favourite women's magazine.

I found I couldn't concentrate on the short story or the serials, but one of the features caught my attention, simply because it was written by a well-known astrologer, and astrology, as I'd admitted to Ran, was a subject that rather intrigued me. Even if it was all nonsense at least it was amusing nonsense—and sometimes it also held an uncanny ring of truth.

The article I was reading, for instance, attempted to sum up the principal characteristics of the people born under the various signs of the zodiac and I could recognise my father as a typical Arian and my mother as a Piscean. Wrinkling my brow, I tried to remember the date of Ran's birthday. November the eighteenth ... that made him a Scorpio, I thought triumphantly.

'Scorpio people can be secretive and enigmatic. They are also intense and passionate, but they hold their feelings inside their hearts and rarely show their real emotions.'

The words seemed to leap out at me from the printed page and I smiled a little wryly. How true that was of Ran! I would never have guessed, if it hadn't been for Kit, that he was still carrying a torch for Venetia ... another man's wife.

The sun was shining with late afternoon brilliance when we touched down at Athens and I felt excitement catch me by the throat. I had been abroad before but this was different. This was Greece ... a land old and strange, that I'd heard about for years.

Ran made several telephone calls from the airport and, true to his promise, did his best to contact Kit. He phoned his flat without success and though he tried one or two numbers, each time he drew a blank.

'Sorry, Annabel,' he said to me. 'I'm afraid it looks as though Kit is still in Salonika.'

I nodded. 'Yes. Thank you for trying, Ran.'

I was disappointed but not, perhaps, as disappointed as Ran thought I was. I would have liked to have seen Kit, but with my first glimpse of Piraeus

I'm ashamed to say that I forgot all about him. There was so much else to occupy my attention. The harbour was crowded with craft of all kinds—caiques, pleasure yachts and cruise steamers—and people of many nationalities. The noise of shouts, singing and ships' sirens was deafening.

'Is that the *Ariadne*? Oh, Ran, is that it?' Tamsin squealed as Ran steered us towards a beautiful motor yacht with immaculate white bows, and Ran laughed.

'Not "it", Tamsin. Boats are always females: you should say "her".'

At the sound of our voices a short, stocky little man wearing a white starched drill jacket had come hurrying on deck, a smile creasing his swarthy features as Ran raised his hand in greeting.

'That's Niko, the steward. He's been with my uncle for many years,' Ran said to me as we stepped on to the gangplank. 'He's Greek, of course, but you'll find that he speaks quite good English and so does his wife, Sia. She's the cook.'

'*Kalispera*.' Still beaming, Niko greeted us enthusiastically and I realised that he and Ran were old friends. Doubtless Ran had been a guest on the *Ariadne* many times before: he had always been fonder of the sea than Kit, who in that sense at least was a traitor to his Greek blood.

Ran exchanged a few words with Niko and then turned to Tamsin and me.

'First of all I'll show you your cabins and you may like to unpack your things. Then, when you're ready, you can join me in the saloon and I'll show you over the rest of the boat and introduce you to the crew.'

'Is it a large one?' I asked, and Ran shook his head.

'No. Apart from Niko and Sia, there are only two others: Matheos, the skipper, and his nephew, Spiro, who's the engineer.'

'Oh, it's lovely! I didn't think it would be as lovely as this!' Tamsin, who had been gazing around her with eager eyes, gave a little skip of excitement which earned her an admonitory glance from Ran.

'Don't get too carried away, Tamsin! You'll be falling overboard next and I don't particularly want to have to dive into the Aegean to rescue you!' he said teasingly.

'You would though, wouldn't you?' she asked, seizing hold of his hand and giving him such a loving, trustful smile that I couldn't help catching my breath.

'No, I wouldn't! I'd leave you to drown!' Ran retorted, ruffling her hair. 'Father Neptune would grill your toes and have them on toast for supper!'

Tamsin giggled. 'Silly! There isn't such a person as Father Neptune, is there, Annabel?'

'No, but I think if I were you I'd be pretty careful, just the same,' I said, aware even as I spoke that my own excitement was bubbling through my voice and that if I looked in a mirror I would probably see it dancing in my eyes as well.

Ran gave the keys of the car to Niko so that he could fetch our luggage and then led the way below deck. I had imagined that my cabin would be little more than a tiny cubicle, but in actual fact it was a luxuriously appointed twin-bedded stateroom, decorated in pale blue, with plenty of fitted storage space and an adjoining shower. Tamsin's cabin was a little smaller, but it was just as comfortable and she was obviously charmed with it.

Sia, Niko's plump, bright-eyed little wife, appeared and offered to help me to unpack, but I told her that we could manage. I started first on Tamsin's suitcases, which were pale blue leather embossed with her initials. The clothes they contained were beautiful—impeccably tailored little trouser suits, colourful cotton dresses and a swimsuit for every day of the week. All in all, I thought rather wryly, she had a very much more extensive wardrobe than mine, and certainly a far more expensive one. Only ...

Tamsin watched me gravely as I knelt on the floor, shaking the creases out of a sunflower-yellow dress that I knew would look lovely with her nut-brown hair and eyes. At any rate, I thought, Venetia showed some interest in her stepdaughter's appearance, though perhaps since she herself was a model that was the least one could expect!

'Don't bother to hang everything up! You've got your own things to unpack,' Tamsin protested, and I gave her a reassuring smile.

'That won't take long. I haven't brought very much.'

'You're not like Venetia, then. Daddy always says her excess baggage costs him a small fortune,' Tamsin remarked, then looked suddenly thoughtful. 'Goodness, I wonder if *that*'s why he doesn't take her away with him any more? He always used to, but now whenever he has to go abroad he goes by himself.'

I was startled but tried not to show it. 'Someone has to look after you, Tamsin——'

'That's what we had Françoise for,' Tamsin protested. She paused, then added in a dignified voice which made me suppress an involuntary chuckle,

'Anyway, I can look after myself. I'm quite sensible, you know.'

'I'm sure you are,' I agreed.

Unexpectedly Tamsin sighed. 'Sometimes I think I'm a bit more sensible than Venetia. She cries such a lot, and whenever I ask her what's the matter she just shakes her head and says "Nothing". It isn't sensible to cry for nothing, is it?' She paused again, then added sadly, 'Ran's the only person who can make her cheer up. I can't, though I do try.'

I bit my lip. 'Tamsin, my poppet, I don't think you ought to talk to me about your stepmother. She— she might not like it——'

Tamsin stared at me. 'But I'm not saying anything horrid about her!' she protested. 'I wouldn't, Annabel, not *ever*! I—I love Venetia, I really do! It's just —I can't help wishing she was like she used to be when she first married Daddy. She was always happy, and so was Daddy. But now——' She stopped.

But now Venetia had found that she had made a mistake—that she had married the wrong man after all? The thought came unbidden into my mind, but almost instantly I pushed it away.

Firmly I said, 'Perhaps she's not very well, Tamsin —perhaps she's been working too hard and she needs a holiday. Perhaps after a fortnight in Crete she'll feel a whole lot better.'

Tamsin's small, heart-shaped face lit up. 'Yes, perhaps she will.' She flung her arms around me and gave me a sudden hug. 'Oh, Annabel, you are nice! I *am* glad you're here, and not Françoise!'

'Good heavens, are you two still unpacking?' Ran's deep voice spoke from the doorway and I turned to find him laughing down at me. He had changed into a pair of jeans and a faded cheesecloth shirt and looked more relaxed than I had ever seen him.

'I've come to tell you that dinner, for us, will be in an hour's time,' he told me. 'Sia is going to give Tamsin something to eat directly I've shown you both over the boat.' He smiled at his goddaughter. 'Sia thinks you must be tired after your long journey and that you'd probably like to go to bed a little earlier than usual. We're sailing first thing tomorrow morning.'

I looked at Tamsin, half expecting indignant protests, but none were forthcoming and I suddenly realised that she did indeed look worn out. She had had a long day, and a lot of excitement.

Feeling that Ran was anxious to get the tour of inspection over I decided to leave my own unpacking until later and followed him and Tamsin to the saloon. This had luxuriously cushioned seats, a soft, thick, fitted carpet and pine-panelled walls hung with old parchment maps. Next Ran showed us the dining saloon, his own cabin, which was the twin of mine, another smaller cabin and the galley, where Sia was preparing vegetables.

Despite her tiredness Tamsin wanted to see everything, including the engine room and the crew's quarters, but eventually she was satisfied and reluctantly consented to eat her supper and get ready for bed. I hurried her along as much as I could, then kissed her goodnight and joined Ran in the saloon for a pre-dinner drink.

'Everything all right?' he asked, handing me a long,

frosted glass in which ice cubes tinkled like little silver bells. 'Your cabin's quite comfortable—you have everything you need? And Tamsin isn't being too much of a nuisance?'

I smiled and shook my head. 'Tamsin isn't being a nuisance at all. In fact, I think she's a darling.'

Ran studied me thoughtfully over the rim of his glass. 'I rather gather that she's fallen for you, too. Not, of course, that I'm in the least surprised,' he added, a faint smile touching his lips.

I went pink. 'You don't have to pay me compliments, you know, Ran. I don't expect you to.'

He looked amused. 'And you don't have to be so prickly!' he retorted. 'I wouldn't pay you any compliments that I didn't mean.'

I could feel my flush becoming deeper. 'Ran, I'm not obtuse. I know you've never really approved of me——'

'I wasn't aware that you were in need of my approval.' Ran spoke drily. 'You never seemed to have time for anyone except Kit.' He paused, then added abruptly, 'You still haven't, have you?'

I bit my lip. 'He's still my best friend, if that's what you mean.'

'I don't, and you know quite well that I don't.' Ran's voice had suddenly sharpened. 'Annabel, don't let Kit hurt you——'

'He never would!' I fired up immediately. 'Never!'

'No?' Ran's mouth went down at one corner. 'Weren't you hurt when he wrote to tell you that he wasn't coming home for Easter after all? Didn't you feel that he'd let you down?'

Wincing—that wound was still raw—I snapped

back at him, 'Kit would have come home if he possibly could! He wanted to see me just as much as I wanted to see him!'

Ran raised his brows. 'You're sure of that?'

'Of course.' I spoke defiantly.

Ran sighed. 'Annabel, why don't you face facts? You and Kit had a lovely boy-and-girl friendship, but it's not the sort that lasts into adult life. You're both bound to take on new and even dearer loyalties——'

'Ran, I'm not going to listen to you!' To my horror I found that my eyes were beginning to blur with angry tears. 'You don't understand anything about Kit and me. You never have!'

Ran sighed. 'You always were as stubborn as a mule——'

'And you always knew all the answers!' I brushed away my tears with the back of my hand, but perhaps Ran saw them, for when he next spoke his voice had changed.

'Oh lord! Annabel, I don't want to fight with you. I've no right to hector you ... I won't do it again, I promise. I'll mind my own business, and leave you to mind yours. Okay?'

I nodded. I was confused, a little ashamed of the fact that I had deliberately let Ran think that my feelings for Kit were stronger than they actually were. 'Okay. I don't want to fight, either. And it certainly wouldn't be good for Tamsin to overhear us——'

Ran's smile was a little twisted. 'I hadn't thought of that. All right. Sweetness and light, Annabel, that's the order of the day from now on——'

I shook my head, laughing in spite of myself. 'I

don't think we ought to expect miracles! You and I have always rubbed each other up the wrong way—always wrangled——'

'But bad habits can be broken.' Ran's eyes held a gleam of laughter. 'Let's try to forget old enmities, shall we . . . try to be friends?'

Friends! I was aware of an odd, almost enjoyable misery. 'Yes, let's,' I agreed, my voice stilted.

'Good. We'll drink to that, shall we?' said Ran, and raised his glass and smiled. A warm glow seemed to spread from my toes to every part of me. Perhaps he really did like me a little after all, I thought humbly, and raised my own glass just as Sia came in to tell us that the meal was now ready.

I can't remember now what we ate. Everything was delicious, but I was more conscious of Ran's nearness, the shape of his hand as it lay on the polished surface of the table, the way his hair crisped at the nape of his neck, than the food upon my plate or my unfamiliar surroundings.

We talked of nothing and everything. I told Ran how much I was enjoying my last year at university, despite the hard work involved, and in return he told me all about the six months he had just spent in America, working at the famous Palomar Observatory with its two-hundred-inch reflecting telescope.

I kept my eyes on his face. Hypnotised by the magic of his voice, I forgot I had never been much interested in astronomy. Ran made it all sound wonderful . . . exciting. Black holes . . . red giants . . . white dwarfs . . . they were names, I thought dreamily, that were guaranteed to stir even the most sluggish imagination!

'I wish I knew more about what you've been talking about!' I exclaimed when Sia brought in the dessert, and Ran laughed.

'If you really mean that, I've a book somewhere that I bought for Tamsin.' Then as I smiled somewhat ruefully he added hastily, 'It's basic, of course, but not *too* basic! That's why I haven't given it to Tamsin yet—at the moment it's still way above her head.'

'I'd like to read it. Thank you,' I said.

'Tell me if you're still interested when you've finished it. If you are we'll have a night's star-gazing,' he said, smiling, and I caught my breath.

Star-gazing . . . with Ran? Well, why not? I asked myself defiantly. It certainly wouldn't be a romantic assignment, not when the two people involved were Ran and me.

I awoke next morning to the throb of the *Ariadne*'s twin five-hundred-horsepower diesel engines in my ears and when I looked out of my porthole there was nothing to be seen but a dawn-lit sea that seemed to have the milky translucence of moonstones.

Tamsin was still fast asleep, curled up in a tight little ball, so I didn't wake her. Instead I scrambled into jeans and a butcher-blue shirt, rinsed my face and hands, ran a comb through my hair and then made my way on deck. The first person I saw was Ran, leaning over the rails.

'Hello, early bird.' He turned his head and gave me the smile which always transformed him from a man who was merely handsome into someone completely devastating. 'Couldn't you sleep?'

'I heard the engines. Where are we heading for?'

'Cape Sounion and the Temple of Poseidon,' Ran told me. 'With any luck we'll be there by breakfast time and thus beat the usual polyglot crowds of tourists.'

He was right, and we were. We breakfasted in Port Sounion with the temple bright above us, its pure white columns dazzling against the deep blue sky as in the days of Byron, who, Ran told me, had carved his name into the marble.

'Byron and graffiti . . . what an odd combination!' I said with a grimace when, later, we were standing by the great marble columns and staring seawards. I couldn't help thinking of all those ancient Greek mariners who had visited this temple in the hope of placating the mighty god of the sea before embarking upon their perilous voyages, and maybe Ran was thinking of them, too. At any rate I saw him put his hand into his pocket and, a moment later, a coin spinning through the air.

'When sailing these seas maybe it's just as well to pay some small observance to the old gods,' he said, and I laughed.

'Ran, you're a scientist! You can't possibly believe in things like old gods——'

'I've got Greek blood, remember?' I couldn't tell from Ran's face whether he was serious or pulling my leg. 'The Greeks absorb their ancient myths with their mothers' milk, and if any sea can be said to be myth-haunted, then it's the Aegean!'

Tamsin, less interested in the past than in the immediate present, pulled at his sleeve.

'How far away is the nearest island?'

'Kea? About twenty miles, but we're not going to

drop anchor there, Tamsin. Our first port of call will be Kythnos,' Ran told her. 'Look—it's here.'

He pulled a somewhat crumpled map from his pocket and while he and Tamsin were studying it I stepped to the edge of the rock-strewn cliff to gaze, entranced, across still blue sea to a distant island. It wouldn't have surprised me, somehow, to have seen one of the frail caiques of bygone days riding the waves, but there was nothing but the flicker of a white sail.

Below me was a patch of yellow and blue flowers. I leant over a little further to try to identify them and as I did so a pebble dislodged itself beneath my foot. Suddenly I heard a movement behind me and turning, I felt Ran's arms go around me roughly, pulling me towards him, away from the edge.

'Never do that again!' he said sharply. 'Never stand so close to the edge of a cliff! You can't possibly know how safe it is——'

He stopped abruptly and I was suddenly aware of the tension in his body and the sound and sensation of his quick-drawn breath. My heart began to thud. For a moment we stared into each other's eyes and then Ran abruptly let me go.

His voice was not quite steady when he said, 'I always used to think it was Kit who egged you on to take silly risks, Annabel, but maybe I was wrong. Maybe you've got no more sense than he has——'

I was furious. 'I was perfectly safe! There was no need for you to grab hold of me like that!' I flashed. Those first words were uttered in a rather shaky voice, but I managed to control the next. 'For goodness' sake, Ran, you might try to remember that I'm no longer a child——'

Ran looked at me, a blaze in his dark eyes that might—or might not—have been anger, and muttered something almost unintelligible under his breath before stalking off to rejoin Tamsin. They walked down the hillside hand in hand, and I followed just behind them, still smarting. And wondering, too, if I really had heard Ran say 'As if I'm in any danger of forgetting *that*!' or whether I'd just imagined it.

CHAPTER THREE

'I THINK I'd probably be quite happy to stay here for ever,' I said lazily, rolling on to my stomach. The *Ariadne* had arrived at Andros and although Ran had stayed aboard to help Matheos with some small problem that was causing him anxiety Tamsin and I had been lucky enough to find ourselves a secluded bay where we could swim and sunbathe. It was completely deserted save for us and some seabirds soaring high and free, and for once there was no wind with an edge to it—the strong *meltemi*, which blew nearly every day from the north-east—to spoil the relaxing warmth of the sunbaked sand.

'Mmm. It's a nice island, but don't forget we haven't seen many yet,' Tamsin said cautiously. 'I like it better than Kythnos, though, don't you?'

I hesitated. Harsh, mountainous Kythnos had been rather a shock in some ways: it certainly wasn't a romantic island. And yet there had been something oddly restful about its air of timelessness. The inhabitants of Kythnos, one felt, would never need psychiatrists or tranquillisers, though even there we'd heard the click of the inevitable amber-coloured worry beads—the Greek panacea for restless hands.

'I don't know,' I said thoughtfully. 'It had something, you know, Tamsin.'

'The mules were fun.' Tamsin giggled reminiscently. 'Much better than motor cars! It was awfully funny when you fell off yours, Annabel.'

'You horrid child!' I pretended to be indignant.

'I wouldn't have laughed if you'd hurt yourself,' Tamsin said hastily. 'Though Ran didn't laugh at all, did he? Not even when he knew you were all right.'

I felt my cheeks grow warm as I remembered how worried Ran had been and how gentle his hands as he'd made sure that I had no broken bones. It had been his idea in the first place that we should hire the mules, for we'd been anxious to visit the village of Kythnos, which lay about a mile and a half inland, and the only route had been a mule-track, jagged with stones. It had been a worthwhile journey, however, for I felt I should never forget the sparklingly clean streets where even the pavements were whitewashed and the little *taverna* where for a few drachmas we had drunk fresh lemon juice and eaten big chunks of bread with goat's cheese and olives.

Intrigued by a way of life that I guessed had hardly changed since the siege of Troy, I had been sorry to leave Kythnos, but this island—Andros—had so much charm that I was filled with anticipation for what must come next. The joy of cruising in the Cyclades, Ran had told me, was that no island was quite like another: each had its own individual personality.

I dragged my eyes from a small fishing caïque and tried to concentrate on what Tamsin was saying.

'Perhaps you'll be able to buy some postcards here, Annabel. You did say you wanted some, didn't you?' And then, as I nodded, 'Who are you going to send them to? Your mother and father?'

'Of course. I promised to keep in touch.'

Tamsin sighed. 'I'd like to send some postcards, too, but I don't know where Daddy and Venetia are staying,' she said rather wistfully. 'I wish they didn't both have to go away so much. It was bad enough when it was just Daddy, but now Venetia doesn't seem to want to stay at home either——'

'She probably doesn't have much choice in the matter,' I said gently, and Tamsin sighed.

'It's all so different from what I thought it was going to be like! Venetia told me, when she first married Daddy, that we'd have a house in the country and we'd have a dog for Daddy and a pony for me and a baby for Venetia. But it hasn't worked out like that——'

The sudden misery in her big brown eyes alarmed me. I said quickly, 'Tamsin, houses in the country are very expensive. Maybe your Daddy can't afford it yet——'

Tamsin shook her head. 'He can. It's just that he and Venetia have changed their minds, I think. Annabel——'

'Yes?'

'Can I tell you something? Something terribly private?'

I hesitated, but I could not harden myself against the imploring look on Tamsin's face.

'Yes, if you really want to. I won't tell anyone else.'

'Not even Ran?'

I permitted myself a slightly rueful smile. Obviously Tamsin thought that Ran and I were closer than we really were. Certainly we laughed and joked together as though we were the best of friends, but all the time I was conscious that even if our relationship was no longer spiced with antagonism there was still a barrier between us—a barrier that I could never break down.

'Not even Ran?' Tamsin repeated anxiously, and I shook my head.

'No. Not even Ran.'

Tamsin's big eyes slid sideways from mine and she plaited her fingers nervously. 'Daddy and Venetia don't like each other any more.' The words came out in a breathless little rush. 'I'm sure they don't. They—they're always arguing. They try not to do it in front of me, but I know they want to—I can tell from their faces. It—it's horrid, Annabel, I hate it——'

I swallowed hard. 'Tamsin, I'm afraid that husbands and wives do argue sometimes, but it doesn't mean that they—that they don't like each other any more or that there's anything really wrong——'

'Françoise thinks there's something wrong,' Tamsin said miserably. 'I heard her telling someone. Of course, she didn't know I was listening——'

I took a deep breath, knowing that on no account must I let Tamsin see how dismayed I was by her revelations.

'You probably misunderstood Françoise, Tamsin— or she herself had somehow got hold of the wrong end of the stick. It—it's very easy to make a mountain out of a molehill, you know. If I were you I'd stop worrying——'

'I can't help it, when I know quite well that Daddy and Venetia are unhappy,' Tamsin protested, and I put my arm around her shoulders.

'Listen, Tamsin, being married isn't easy,' I said gently. 'Everybody has to learn to make adjustments and sometimes that takes quite a long time. Maybe Venetia and your father *are* going through rather a bad patch just now, but you've got to have faith in them. They—they wouldn't have married each other if they hadn't loved each other very much, you know. You said yourself how happy they were to begin with——'

Tamsin nodded. 'Yes. But I wish—I wish Daddy and Venetia were both coming to Crete, not just Venetia. Then I'd know that everything was all right, really——'

I gave her a swift hug. 'Everything *is* all right,' I told her, and perhaps I sounded more confident than I really felt, for her face lightened. Her change of expression made me feel that perhaps a change of subject was indicated, too, and I sat up.

'What do you think that funny pink blob is over there? Do you suppose it's a jellyfish?'

'I'll go and see, shall I?' Tamsin asked, jumping to her feet.

'Yes, but for heaven's sake don't touch it!'

I watched her run across the sand, my thoughts sombre. If only I could tell Ran how troubled Tamsin was about the relationship between her father and her beautiful young stepmother! But of course I couldn't. Apart from the fact that I'd hate to break my promise to Tamsin, there were other reasons why it was impossible to do so.

'It is a jellyfish, but it's dead.' Tamsin came flying back to me. 'I can see Ran coming: shall we go to meet him?'

'I'm quite comfortable where I am. You've got more energy than I have: you go,' I told her, and realised with amazement that I had been smitten by self-consciousness. Ran had never seen me in a bikini before and though I wasn't shy of him—of course I wasn't—I intended to stay where I was, hugging my knees and staring at the sea, which sparkled in bands of jewel-like colour.

'Hi.' Ran, with Tamsin clinging tightly to his hand, came up behind me. 'Have you had a swim? What was the water like?'

'Marvellous,' I said, and looked up at him as he stood there smiling, his dark eyes narrowed against the brightness of the sun.

'Why don't you try it for yourself?' Tamsin suggested, but Ran shook his head.

'I'm going into Andros to buy some supplies for Sia. She isn't feeling too well, else of course she'd go herself. I thought if you two could bear to tear yourselves away from this rather delectable beach you might like to come with me.'

'Oh yes, please,' Tamsin said eagerly, and looked at me. 'Perhaps you'll be able to buy your postcards, Annabel.'

Ran fished in his pocket. 'I've got a list here that Sia gave me. Luckily it's not a very long one—her handwriting is even worse than mine!'

Shopping in Greece was, as Tamsin and I had already both agreed, far more fun than shopping in an English supermarket, but it also took far longer, and by the time we had finished it was late afternoon.

'I don't think I shall be in a hurry to offer to help in this way again,' Ran said ruefully when we returned to the *Ariadne*. 'Oh—did you get the melons, Annabel? And the cheese?'

'I did. I'm getting quite to like goat's cheese, though I didn't think I would.'

'What about Greek cuisine generally?' Ran looked at me quizzically and I laughed.

'I like that, too. I've probably put on pounds already!'

Tamsin pulled a face. 'You sound just like Venetia! Why do grown-ups worry all the time about getting fat?' she grumbled.

'I can tell you why Venetia does. Nobody would want to photograph her if she were fat and ugly, would they?' Ran asked seriously.

'She couldn't ever be! Not Venetia!' Tamsin exclaimed, looking shocked. 'I wish—oh, I do wish I could grow up to look just like her! She's so beautiful! Do you know, she had four proposals before she decided to marry Daddy? *Four!*' She sighed. 'I guess I'll be lucky if I get just one!'

Her expression was comical, but I didn't laugh. Nor did Ran. His face was impassive, but I was afraid that if I looked into his eyes I would see them become suddenly shadowy, haunted. Because though of course Tamsin didn't know it, his proposal must have been one of the four that Venetia had turned down.

Anchored in a small bay, we lay two nights off Andros, the days all sunlight, hot sand and blue skies, the sea sparkling with whitecaps. We swam, sunbathed and made friends with the hospitable islanders, who seemed genuinely sorry when Ran decided that it was time we moved on to Delos and Mykonos. Apparently he had friends staying on Mykonos, people who lived for most of the year in Athens but

who had a summer villa overlooking one of the
island's most beautiful bays.

'I'm specially looking forward to Delos,' I told
Tamsin. 'Do you know the legend about it? It was a
wandering island until Poseidon struck it with his
trident and anchored it firmly to the bed of the sea so
that the goddess Leto could give birth to Apollo. Immediately he was born all the surface of the island
was transformed into a carpet of flowers——'

I broke off, suddenly aware that Ran was laughing.

'You're a romantic young woman, aren't you?
Funny, I would never have suspected it. I always
thought you were pretty hard-boiled, like Kit——'

'You shouldn't stick labels on people. I'm not hard-
boiled, but I don't think I'm particularly romantic,
either.'

'Of course you are. I wouldn't mind betting that
you like *Clare de Lune* and Tennyson's *Princess*
and *The Lord of the Rings* and that somewhere
you've got a box of precious keepsakes. All Kit's letters tied up with a piece of blue ribbon, old photographs ... maybe even a ring out of a Christmas
cracker ...'

'I haven't! I haven't got anything like that!' I said
indignantly, stung by the mockery I could see in his
eyes.

'You're sure?'

'Of course! At least——' I stopped abruptly. It was
true that I'd never kept anything to remind me of Kit,
but I did have a tiny photograph of Ran in a Victorian
silver locket that had once belonged to my grand-
mother. And at one time—before Venetia appeared

on the scene—I'd worn that locket practically day
and night . . .

'You see?' There was an odd note in Ran's voice. 'I
was right.'

I didn't answer. I don't know what he saw in my
flushed face, but whatever it was it caused his own
expression to change.

'I'm sorry. I suppose—you're missing Kit rather
badly. Aren't you?'

'Of course not!' I spoke sharply—too sharply.
'I'm having too good a time to worry about missing
anyone! You say I'm romantic. Well, this trip is a
fairytale come true——'

'Not really a fairytale, since it lacks the essential
ingredient.' Ran's voice was dry.

'The essential ingredient?'

Ran raised his brows. 'Prince Charming, of course.'

'Your humility becomes you.' I spoke sarcastically
and Ran gave me an ironical bow.

'On the contrary, my dear Annabel. It's because I
lack humility that I strongly object to playing a surrogate role!'

'I don't know what you two are talking about,'
Tamsin complained. 'Annabel, I'm thirsty. Can I go
and ask Sia for some fruit juice, please?'

'Of course. I'm thirsty, too: I'll come with you.'

I turned to her quickly, glad of the chance to escape. Lightly though Ran's last words had been
spoken, I sensed that they had held nothing of amusement. Why did he veer so unexpectedly between
warmth and hostility? No, not hostility, that wasn't
the right word. But certainly in his dark eyes just
then there had been something very far removed

from the superficial lightness of our conversation.

Sia was making *pakclava*, a delicious syrup-covered almond pastry that Tamsin loved. Sia was obviously very fond of children and spoke often of her large family of sons and daughters, now all grown up and married.

'Sia says she's sorry for me because I'm an only child,' Tamsin remarked as carrying our glasses of fruit juice we rejoined Ran on the upper deck. 'I think I'm rather sorry for me, too. It must be lovely to have lots of brothers and sisters to play with.'

I laughed. 'I used to say that sort of thing when I was your age, Tamsin. Remember that I was an only child, too.'

'But you had Ran and Kit,' Tamsin protested. 'They were sort of brothers, weren't they?'

'I suppose they were——' I began, but Ran interrupted me.

'Oh no!' he said emphatically, shaking his head. 'I can't speak for Kit, of course, but I can assure you that at no time have I ever felt like Annabel's elder brother, Tamsin.'

'But suppose she marries Kit! She *will* be your sister then, won't she—your sister-in-law!' Tamsin exclaimed triumphantly, and I felt my cheeks burn.

Ran cast a brief glance in my direction, then shrugged his shoulders. 'I don't think we'll bother with suppositions, Tamsin.'

'But you said——'

'Let's drop the subject, shall we?' Ran frowned at his goddaughter, then turned to me. 'That's your enchanted island over there, Annabel. At the moment it's almost certainly teeming with tourists, so I don't think we'll bother to land until we can be reasonably sure that they've all gone. I don't suppose we'll have too long to wait.'

A wild stab of delight shot through me as the island came in sight, its ancient ruins looking almost unreal against the cobalt blue sky. I was glad that Ran seemed to feel the same way as I did about crowds. Maybe it was greedy of us to want to have the whole island to ourselves, but I had already discovered that myth and magic did not walk hand-in-hand with the whirr of cameras, the toneless monologues of bored guides and the shrill exclamations of tourists jostling each other in order to gain the best possible view.

We anchored in a tiny cove which, hidden away from the rest of the island, was completely deserted. Here the water was clearer than I had ever seen it before and Tamsin and I hung over the bows to stare, entranced, at the illuminated white sand bottom of the sea-bed. Seaweeds moved and swayed in ever-changing patterns of carmine and jade and amber, there were shells everywhere and occasionally a small, darting fish, brightly hued.

Only when the last caiques from Mykonos had departed with their cargoes of visitors did we go ashore in the dinghy to climb through fields of carefully tended vegetables and corn towards the rocky slopes of Mount Cynthus and the Sacred Way, worn by the footsteps of the thousands who in ancient times had come to make offerings and sacrifice to the sun god. We wandered for a long time among the ruins, leaving the Sanctuary of Apollo, a great square impressive in its size and silence, to cross the Sacred Lake and marvel at the famous Lions of Delos, glimmering marble-white in the half-light.

It was at this point that Tamsin became bored and Sia, who had come with us, offered to take her back to the *Ariadne* while Ran and I visited the House of the Trident, the House of Dolphins and the House of Masks.

'You won't see very much,' Tamsin objected. 'It's nearly dark already.'

Ran glanced at the sky, already pricked by faint stars, and shook his head.

'There's a full moon tonight, remember? It will be rising soon and then it'll be as clear as daylight— and twice as romantic!' he added with a teasing glance at me.

I said nothing. Already I was completely under the spell of the past. Ran was right. This was the way to see Delos, not in daytime and in the wake of a guide but when it was night and the island was given back to a silence more potent than speech.

At least . . . silence of a sort, for when Sia and Tamsin had gone Ran and I sat on a crumbling slab of rock and listened to the croaking of innumerable bullfrogs, a sound which made some lines of Edna St Vincent Millay's, learned in childhood, suddenly come back into my mind.

> 'I had forgotten how the frogs must sound
> After a year of silence, else I think
> I should not so have ventured forth alone
> At dusk, upon this unfrequented road.
> I am waylaid by beauty. Who will walk
> Between me and the crying of the frogs?'

It was moonlight now and the whole island seemed

to be drenched with an almost unearthly radiance that blanched the ancient ruins to silver. Everything seemed strangely still and waiting. Waiting—for what?

For what seemed a long time Ran and I sat absolutely still without moving or speaking, but then a moth flew across my face and when I put up my hand to touch it the spell was broken. I sighed and stirred and beside me I heard Ran laugh softly.

'I was beginning to think Apollo had bewitched you, Annabel . . . turned you into a statue.'

A cool breeze caressed my shoulders as he spoke and involuntarily I shivered. The night was warm, but I was wearing only the sleeveless shift that I had worn earlier, in the heat of the day.

'Are you cold?' Ran demanded, and without waiting for my answer he stripped off his jacket and draped it round me. Was it my imagination, or did his hands linger on my shoulders?

'Thank you. But now it's you who'll feel cold——'

'No, I won't.' Ran paused then added almost brusquely, 'Anyway, I rather think it's time we were getting back. Don't you?'.

He put out his hand to draw me to my feet, and at his touch a surge of longing suddenly swept over me. Deliberately I leaned towards him so that my hair brushed his cheek and the sound of his quick-drawn breath throbbed through my veins. Then I felt his hands on my shoulders, drawing me close, and I could hear my heart pounding. Or was it his? I couldn't tell.

'Look at me, Annabel.' It was a command, but one that I could not—would not—obey. I knew quite well that if I looked into his eyes I would see not the love I wanted but simply desire. I could never be anything to Ran but a temporary replacement for a lost love—never.

Gently Ran put his fingers beneath my chin and tilted my face upwards. Then the stars—even the moonlight—were blotted out as his lips came down on mine, gently at first, then fiercely demanding. I knew that I should struggle away from him, but I couldn't. Instead I stood unresisting in his arms, tingling and melting under his lips, arching my body to his hands as they outlined the slope of my shoulders and lingered at my breast, until suddenly, with something that might have been a groan, he pushed me away from him.

'Damn!' he said shakily, stepping back and brushing his hand across his eyes. 'Damn it! I told you I wasn't interested in playing a surrogate Prince Charming——'

'You're not——'

'Annabel, what do you take me for? A fool?' Ran's voice was harsh. 'Come on, let's get back to the ship. You've had your romantic interlude. It's over. Done. Curtain.'

The savagery with which he spoke demolished my dreams. Delos was no longer a magic island and Ran no longer a fairytale prince but a grim-faced man angry with himself because just for a moment he had allowed a seductive setting and his own long-deprived senses to betray him.

Apart, neither of us speaking, we walked back to the shore, where Matheos was waiting for us with the dinghy. There was a nasty, tight feeling at the back of my throat. So often had I imagined myself in Ran's arms, but now that it had finally happened I could not recall the rapture of his embrace, only its bitter aftermath and the anger in his face and voice. What had I done to make him so angry? Did he feel that by kissing me so passionately he had somehow betrayed Venetia? But she wasn't his to betray, and she never would be, now that she was Paul's wife. Unless . . . But I wouldn't think about that. I wouldn't let it even cross my mind!

CHAPTER FOUR

UNTIL Delos I had been looking forward to our arrival on Mykonos with mixed feelings. Ran had made it clear that he hoped to see a lot of his friends, Yanna and Christos Machelevos and their seventeen-year-old daughter Melita, and I felt guilty because I was not more enthusiastic about the prospect. Basically, I suppose, I didn't want to share Ran with anyone—I just wanted it to be him and me and Tamsin.

Now, though, Delos had changed everything. Neither of us referred to that moment of madness when beneath the ghostly ruins of a bygone age he had taken me into his arms and kissed me, but there was a constraint between us that had not been there before and I knew that I was as much to blame for it as Ran himself. I was glad, now, that we would have company on Mykonos. Perhaps by the time we left Ran would feel less guilty and I less miserably aware that I had virtually thrown myself at his head. Thank goodness he thought that because I was missing Kit I had simply been extra susceptible to romantic surroundings and a man's magnetism. Any man's ... even his!

Mykonos was only a few miles from Delos and we arrived just before midday. My first impression was one of dazzling brightness, for against a background of low hills crowned with windmills, all of them with white sails spread and turning merrily in the fresh breeze, houses brilliant with whitewash glittered gem-like under the blazing noonday sun.

'Mykonos is the most whitewashed town in all the islands,' said Ran, laughing as we came closer to the island, and Tamsin and I blinked and then covered our eyes with our hands. 'Don't forget to take your sun-glasses with you when you land. You'll find as you walk through the streets that the glare and razzle-dazzle is almost blinding.'

Much to our delight, Tamsin and I were left to explore the town while Ran contacted his friends. We found not only an abundance of tourist shops selling local materials, pottery and postcards but also lots of churches, some looking just like mounds of white icing, little balconies and quaint, winding staircases, vines trailing, alleys rioting with flowers and everywhere charmingly misshapen, whitewashed houses hung with exotic plants.

'I like Mykonos,' Tamsin approved, her brown eyes sparkling. 'Don't you, Annabel?'

'Yes, it's charming.' I tried to speak enthusiastically, but I was still worrying about the previous night. 'I'm not surprised it's so popular with tourists, are you?'

Tamsin pressed her nose against a shop window full of what Ran usually described as 'tourist bait' and then dragged me inside. She seemed very much taken with a little bracelet set with multi-coloured stones, but on looking in her purse reluctantly decided that she couldn't afford it.

I said nothing, but when her attention was distracted I bought the bracelet for her, and slipped it on to her wrist outside the shop.

'Annabel!' Tamsin's eyes opened wide. 'Oh, you darling! But you shouldn't spend your money on me!'

I laughed and put my arm round her thin shoulders. 'Why shouldn't I? It's fun to give presents to people you like.'

Tamsin looked at me. 'Do you know that's the first time you've laughed this morning, Annabel?' she asked unexpectedly. 'I was beginning to wonder if there was something wrong.' She paused, then added, 'Ran seemed a bit grumpy, too——'

I flushed. 'You're imagining things, Tamsin. There's certainly nothing wrong with me!'

'Ran thinks you're missing Kit, doesn't he? *Are* you, Annabel? Would you really like him to be here?' Tamsin demanded.

'Of course I would but you can't have everything, can you? Nobody can,' I temporised, but Tamsin was not satisfied.

'Are you going to buy Kit a present?' she asked.

'Perhaps.' I smiled a little wryly as I spoke. How would Kit react when he learned that I was holidaying in Greece? I wondered. I had written him a long letter, explaining the reason for Ran's unexpected invitation, but I'd forgotten to post it until a day or two ago and I wasn't sure when he'd receive it.

'What do you think he'd like?' Tamsin persisted, and I laughed and shook my head.

'Oh, I expect I'll find something.' I glanced at my watch. 'Heavens, it's time to meet Ran! Come on, we'll have to hurry or we'll be late.'

Ran was waiting for us on the waterfront, looking handsome but vaguely gangsterish in his dark glasses, almost a stranger. But then hadn't he always been that as far as I was concerned? I thought painfully. His voice, his smile, his height and breadth of shoulder I knew well, but not the man inside.

'Did you see your friends?' I asked politely when Tamsin had finished showing him her new bracelet, and he nodded.

'Yes. At least I saw Christos and Yanna. Melita was out, but I shall see her tonight. So will you, Annabel —we've been invited to dinner.'

'Me, too?' Tamsin asked hopefully.

'No, not you, Tamsin. We'll have to ask Sia to look after you on this occasion, I'm afraid, but don't worry. I'm sure there'll be lots of other opportunities for you to visit the Villa Kiara.'

'Is Melita an "only", like Annabel and me?' Tamsin wanted to know, and again Ran shook his head.

'No. She has an elder sister, Elena, who quite recently got married. The two girls were very close and apparently Melita is missing her badly and feeling very lonely. Perhaps you and Annabel will be able to cheer her up a little.'

'Oh no! Shades of Pollyanna!' I murmured, and was rewarded by a faint twinkle in Ran's eyes before it was replaced by a studious blankness.

My sandal had come undone. I bent to fasten it, my hair swinging forward, but the buckle was awkward and at the wrong angle and I couldn't quite manage it. Ran went down on one knee and did it for me, his fingers brushing against mine.

When we both straightened my pulse was racing, but Ran gave no sign of awareness. He merely said, 'We'd better get back to the *Ariadne* now, don't you think? Yanna and Christos are expecting us for dinner at half-past seven.'

His eyes held mine, black and unreadable, and I was conscious of a swelling pain inside me. I was a fool, I told myself angrily. I had to forget about last night—forget how he had held me in his arms and kissed me as no one had ever kissed me before. It had been wonderful at the time, but now I was left with a bitter taste in my mouth. It served me right, of course, and yet——

'Come on, Annabel!' Tamsin was tugging impatiently at my hand and with a sigh I abandoned my unprofitable thoughts and began planning what I should wear. I didn't feel that an informal dinner party called for anything ultra-elaborate, so in the end I decided to wear one of my favourite dresses even though it was a couple of years old. It hadn't cost a lot, but I knew that its high neckline and narrow trimmings of lace gave it a deliciously prim Victorian look and that the colour—a deep midnight blue—might have been specially designed to enhance my eyes and hair. I hoped that Ran would like it, but he made no comment, only gave me a long thoughtful look which might or might not have signified approval.

The Villa Kiara, where Yanna and Christos Machelevos were staying, was set in extensive grounds, brilliant with flowers and exotic shrubs, and the house—whitewashed like all the others on the island —was very large, with shutters and balconies painted in jade green and walls hung with some trailing scarlet flowers I did not know. Yanna Machelevos, beautiful and stately, and Christos, stocky and pleasant-faced, with greying hair, greeted Ran with immense affection and then welcomed me with a warmth which made me appreciate anew the Greek friendliness towards the stranger.

'This is our daughter, Melita. She has been looking forward to your visit,' Yanna told me, and I found myself smiling into a pair of big black eyes.

'Welcome to Mykonos, Annabel,' said Melita, returning my smile. She was very pretty, with a vivid, irregular betwitching type of prettiness, and in spite of her demure demeanour there was a hint of mischief in her smile and a sparkle in her eyes that made me warm to her immediately. She spoke English very well indeed but had little to say during dinner and I, too, was content to leave most of the conversation to Ran and Yanna and Christos, despite their efforts to include me.

'You like Mykonos, I hope, Miss Conway—Annabel, if you will allow me the privilege?' Christos asked, smiling at me across the polished surface of the long refectory table, and I answered him eagerly.

'Oh yes, indeed! It's fascinating! I especially like the windmills——'

'Ah! Mykonos is famous for its windmills,' said Christos, pouring me some more wine. It was cold and sparkling, with a colour like sunlight. 'You will find them on all the islands, of course, but here they are so beautifully sited that photographs are always being taken of them for use on travel folders about Greece.'

'I think Annabel was rather surprised to find the islands such windy places,' Ran said with a grin, and I laughed and nodded in agreement.

After dinner Yanna and Christos took Ran to one side to show him the plans of an extension they were hoping to have built on to the back of the villa and it was left to Melita to entertain me. She did so in a small sitting room which combined elegance with simplicity and which smelt of the delicate red and white flowers that were in bowls and vases all around. Out of the golden haze of the wine I noticed brightly coloured rugs on a polished wood floor ... very modern paintings ... lots of books and magazines.

'You and Ran ... are you engaged?' Melita asked shyly, handing me a cup of coffee which I almost dropped, I was so taken aback by her question.

'Engaged? Of course not! Whatever makes you think that? I'm with him just to look after his god-daughter. He must have told you about her—Tamsin?'

My voice was sharper than I had intended it to be and Melita flushed uncomfortably.

'I'm sorry! I thought my mother said—but I must have been mistaken.'

'Quite mistaken,' I said firmly. 'I'm—I'm just about the last person Ran would ever want to be engaged to.' I stared out of the window as I spoke. There was a huge moon and the velvety sky was again studded with enormous, brilliant stars, but I knew that tonight, when he took me back to the *Ariadne*, there would be no more kisses to enjoy now, repent of later. We'd both learnt our lesson ...

'He likes you very much, though,' Melita was protesting. 'I can tell by the way he looks at you, Annabel.'

'Oh, rubbish!' It was so absurd that in spite of

myself I began to laugh. 'You're imagining things, Melita. I've known Ran Armitage for—oh, for ever!' I paused, then added, 'And his brother, too.'

'You mean Kit?' Melita asked, and I raised my brows.

'Yes. Do you know him?'

'No, but I have heard Ran speak of him quite often. He worries about him quite a lot, doesn't he?' Melita said quaintly.

'You think so?' I spoke rather drily and Melita looked surprised.

'But of course. He is—how do you say?—Ran's baby brother. Poor Kit, it must be very trying for him,' She sighed. 'Me, I know. I am seventeen— nearly eighteen, but still a child, according to my parents. I love them dearly, but I wish—oh, how I wish that they would allow me a little more freedom! You English girls, you are so lucky——'

I looked at her. Then quietly I said, 'Some people might think you're pretty lucky, too. You've got kind and loving parents, a beautiful home, lovely clothes— plenty of money——'

Melita went pink. 'I suppose I must sound ungrateful,' she admitted. 'But it is so dull here now that my sister has married, Annabel! My parents love the island, but there isn't enough for me to do and I have only one or two friends whose company I really enjoy.' She sighed again. 'Just think, I could have gone to your country! Right now I could be in London——'

'Where it's probably grey and chilly and almost certainly raining!' I said, laughing. 'Melita, you're a goose! No one in her right senses would want to swap this gorgeous island for anywhere else in the world!'

'But you aren't going to stay here very long, are you? You're going to visit some other islands,' Melita pointed out. 'I wouldn't mind doing that. It's just being stuck here on Mykonos for weeks on end that I simply hate!'

'Then you'd better stow away on the *Ariadne*!' I said jokingly, and Melita looked thoughtful.

'It belongs to Ran's uncle, doesn't it? Is it a nice yacht?'

'Yes, beautiful. I think Ran said something about inviting you and your parents to lunch tomorrow, so you'll be able to see it for yourself.'

'That will be nice.' Melita's face still wore its thoughtful expression and she answered me somewhat absently. 'I like boats. We had a yacht ourselves once, when I was little, but my mother suffered quite dreadfully from seasickness so it wasn't really much use to us.'

'Tamsin and I are both good sailors. Just as well, really, because at times the sea has been quite choppy. We haven't been caught in a storm yet, though.'

'That could be quite exciting. A storm at sea, I mean——' Melita began, and I laughed.

'I'm sure you're right, but nevertheless it's an excitement that I'm quite willing to forgo!'

Melita shook her head, the sparkle in her dark eyes belying the innocence of her face. 'Me, I like excitement. The trouble is, I hardly ever get it!'

I suddenly thought of Kit. He liked excitement, too, and that was why, when we were younger, he'd taken so many hair-raising risks and encouraged me to take them, too. I hadn't been worried at the time, but now, in retrospect, I could see how stupidly we'd often behaved. Small wonder that Ran had frequently been exasperated, since more often than not it was he who had been forced to rescue us from the consequences of some of our more dangerous escapades.

'Well, have you enjoyed yourself?' Ran asked when we were on our way back to the *Ariadne* and I nodded.

'Very much. Yanna and Christos are charming and I liked Melita very much, too, though she seems to have rather a chip on her shoulder at present.'

Ran frowned. 'Yanna and Christos say that she complains all the time about being bored. They're really quite worried about her, though they still feel they did the right thing in refusing her permission to visit Europe with her friends. They hope to take her to Paris themselves, later this year——'

I interrupted him. 'It's now they want to worry about, not later! She hasn't got enough to do. She was almost pathetically grateful when I suggested that she might like to go shopping with Tamsin and me tomorrow——'

Ran raised his brows. 'More bracelets?'

I shook my head. 'I thought I'd rather like one of those Greek peasant skirts. I saw some lovely ones in a shop this morning.'

Ran laughed. 'Well, in your case I'd say the peasant weave would be quite a good buy. Usually those raw colours seem to appeal most strongly to those women who should at all costs resist them!'

I thought of the portly American lady I had seen trying on a particularly gaudy skirt and suppressed a smile.

'Yes, I know what you mean but—oh, Ran! Look at that!'

We were approaching the harbour and suddenly I had spotted a caique gliding along the water, brilliantly lit up by a huge flare which was burning in the bows. In the light of the flare two men were starkly silhouetted, each holding in his right hand a long, three-pronged spear which looked rather like Neptune's trident.

'A favourite method of catching fish here in Greece is spearing them by torchlight,' Ran explained. 'The flare attracts the fish and the water is so clear that they can easily be seen.'

'Primitive——'

Ran looked amused. 'Perhaps, but exciting, too, like nearly all primitive pastimes!'

'You mean you've done some light-fishing yourself?'

'I have. I even caught an octopus once—ate it, too.'

'Ugh!'

'Yes, it was an experience I do rather want to forget.' Ran paused, then added deliberately, 'Like last night's.'

My heart seemed to jump into my throat. 'L-last night's?'

'You know what I'm talking about.' Ran's voice was bleak. 'I owe you an apology. Your parents, too. They trusted me——'

'Oh, Ran!' I laughed with false amusement. 'It wasn't important! There's really no need to worry. For heaven's sake, I have been kissed before, you know!'

There was a small silence, then Ran said, 'Kit, of course.'

'Well, of course,' I agreed. It wasn't really a lie, I told myself. Kit *had* kissed me. Admittedly I'd been about ten the last time—we'd been playing Postman's Knock at someone's birthday party—but Ran wasn't to know that.

His face, in the moonlight, was granite-hard. 'Well, at least you now have another area in which to compare me with my brother. No doubt it will, as usual, be to my disadvantage!' he said harshly.

I had no chance to reply, for by this time we had reached the *Ariadne* and Niko, leaning over the port-rails, hailed us immediately we came into view. We boarded the yacht in silence and once on deck Ran did not suggest a nightcap, as he usually did, but merely thanked me for my company and said goodnight.

I looked in on Tamsin, who was sleeping peacefully, and then made my way to my own cabin, though it was a long time before I went to sleep. Instead I lay thinking over the events of the evening and puzzling over the bitter flavour of Ran's last remark. Was he perhaps jealous of Kit? It had certainly seemed remarkably like it, yet I found it almost impossible to believe. It was Kit who, when we were younger, had always been jealous of Ran, and I couldn't for the life of me see why the tables should be turned now!

I sighed as I put out the light and lay watching the stars. Would I ever understand what made Ran tick? And—more to the point—would I ever be able to stop loving him?

*

Tamsin was as enchanted with Mykonos as I was, for it seemed that every day there was something new to surprise and delight us. The weather continued to be glorious and we bathed a good deal, quite often three or four times a day. Melita was usually with us and sometimes Ran. We often went to the Villa Kiara for lunch and Melita was our guide whenever we wanted to explore the island. It was, I thought, in danger of being over-commercialised, but it had so many charming features, and Melita herself was such an enchanting companion, that the days passed like a lovely golden dream.

'Must you really go?' Yanna asked regretfully when at last Ran announced the date of our departure. 'We would all be very happy if you could stay longer.'

Ran smiled but shook his head. 'We have to be in Crete by the twenty-seventh and there are one or two other islands I'd like to visit en route. This has been a very pleasant interlude, though: we've all enjoyed it. Haven't we, Annabel?'

'Very much.' I spoke warmly. With the exception of Christos we were all sitting on the terrace of the Villa Kiara, with Tamsin curled up in a big wicker chair reading a book and the rest of us looking out on to the misty blue of the bay where the sails of yachts gleamed like gliding pyramids of white. The sky was a deeper blue—cobalt—and a blue wave of wistaria cascaded over the stone balustrade in front of us.

Yanna looked at Tamsin and smiled. 'What are you reading, Tamsin? It must be exciting: you haven't spoken a word for nearly an hour!'

'It's called *Myths and Legends of Ancient Greece*.

I thought I ought to know a bit more about all those gods and goddesses Ran and Annabel are always talking about,' Tamsin explained seriously. She paused, then wrinkling her nose she added, 'They were a funny lot, weren't they? They were always falling in love with people they shouldn't have fallen in love with at all, and changing themselves into all kinds of different shapes——'

I laughed. 'Yes, they were pretty good at that,' I agreed. 'It was a useful trick, though, Tamsin.'

'It must have been. They didn't ever have to feel bored with being gods and goddesses, did they?' Tamsin propped her chin on her small sunburnt hands. Then unexpectedly she asked, 'Who would you like to be if you weren't you, Annabel?'

'Oh, Tamsin, what a question! I've never really thought about it. Just at this moment I'm more than happy to be me——'

'But if you *had* to choose to be somebody—or something—else?' Tamsin persisted, and I heard Ran chuckle.

'It's no good, Annabel. I'm afraid you're in the hot seat.'

I looked at him, tall and lithe and deeply tanned, his eyes smiling and the lines of his mouth softened attractively, and I felt my heart ache. I wanted to say, 'Venetia. That's who I'd like to be, because she's the only woman you've ever really loved.' Then I realised that I wouldn't, after all, like to be in Venetia's shoes. I'd never want to have to live with the knowledge that I'd made a mistake and married the wrong man . . .

Perhaps Melita, sitting beside me, sensed something

of my momentary despair, for suddenly she put her hand over mine.

'What's the matter? Suddenly you look so sad——'

I answered her quickly, my eyes on Yanna's big grey cat, Quinta, who was basking in the sun.

'I was thinking. Quinta—yes, I'd like to be Quinta, Tamsin. A spoilt and pampered beauty, basking in the sun all day and doubtless living it up all night——'

Tamsin giggled as Quinta turned her head and gave me a long disdainful stare, then rose to her feet, stretched and walked away.

'Oh, Annabel! Now you've offended her!'

'So I should think. Fancy using a revolting phrase like "living it up" in connection with an aristocrat like Quinta!' Ran mocked.

'I wonder how she got her name?' Tamsin looked enquiringly at Yanna, who laughed.

'It means "the fifth". She was the fifth kitten to be born.'

'I can't help wondering what Quinta's other two names are,' I said pensively, and Tamsin looked puzzled.

'What other two names? She's only got one— Quinta!'

'According to a very famous English poet all cats have three names, one for everyday use, one for special occasions and one to be kept a secret,' I explained, and Ran turned to look at me, his eyes holding more of warmth than I had seen for some days.

'T. S. Eliot and *The Naming of Cats*. It's a poem that's given me a good deal of pleasure: I like cats,' he said.

'Me, too.' I smiled at him foolishly, happily, bask-

ing in his approval. I was filled with an unaccustomed
content. I felt as though I wouldn't mind at all if time
suddenly stood still and I had to spend the rest of my
life sitting on this sun-dappled terrace where there
was warmth and quiet, the heart-stirring blueness of
sea and sky, the scent of herbs and something of Ran's
old friendliness towards me.

It was such a wonderful, golden, sunlit world that
I couldn't believe the spell would ever be broken, but
I was wrong. Suddenly the peace was rudely shattered
by the sounds of hissing and screeching. Somewhere
a small war was being waged.

Ran was on his feet, moving with the easy grace
that always gave me a strange curling sensation in
my stomach. 'Cat fight,' he said coolly.

'Quinta! Oh, Quinta!' Yanna rushed to his side and
followed by Tamsin they ran down the steps to where
Quinta was crouched by a bush, her body swollen to
half again her usual size and shaking with menacing
growls. Her enemy was invisible: probably it had
retreated behind the bush.

I was in the act of pushing back my chair when
Melita said, 'No need for us to get involved, Annabel.
Leave it to Ran.'

Reluctantly I sank back into my chair, my eyes
fixed on Ran. He had picked up the squirming, swear-
ing bundle that was Quinta and was gently stroking
her fur. He might talk tough at times, I thought, smiling to myself, but he had a surprisingly kind heart.

A thought drifted up from the depths of my sub-
conscious mind and suddenly I stiffened. Suppose Ran
had tried to be kind to *me*? Suppose he hadn't invited me to accompany him to Greece because he

needed help with Tamsin ... suppose that instead he'd merely been trying to soothe my wounded feelings, the way he was now trying to soothe Quinta's!

Luckily Melita did not allow me long to indulge in such disturbing reflections. Examining a broken fingernail, she said, 'So you're really leaving Mykonos tomorrow?'

'If Ran doesn't change his mind, and I don't suppose he will.' I hesitated, then added, 'We'll miss you, Melita.'

'I'll miss you, too,' Melita said, but so absently that I was both surprised and relieved. I had been rather afraid that she would be very upset about our impending departure, but oddly enough she was smiling, a small, secret smile that somehow seemed to hold a hint of mischief.

'What island are you visiting next? Do you know?' she asked.

'Naxos, I think. Then Ios, then Santorin, and finally Crete.'

'Crete ... that's where Tamsin's stepmother is joining you, isn't it?'

'Yes.'

Melita gave me a sharp look. 'Don't you like her?'

'Venetia? Goodness, I hardly know her,' I said lightly.

'Tamsin seems to be very fond of her. I suppose Ran is, too?' Melita probed.

'I expect so. Paul—Tamsin's father—is his best friend.' I rose to my feet. 'What about a swim, Melita? It's awfully hot: I'd like to cool off.'

The subject of Venetia was dropped, as I'd hoped it would be. We swam then and again later that evening, when it was almost dark. It was a wonderful experience, floating in the warm sea, with the moon shining softly over the scene, and I had some moments of regret because we were not staying in Mykonos longer. In fact, I almost wished that something would happen to delay our departure.

Yanna's cook, Eleni, prepared a farewell banquet for us that evening, but I don't remember the food, just the candles and the flowers and the smell of the wine, sweet and heavy. I drank more of it than I should have done and I thought perhaps Melita had, too, for her pale cheeks were unusually flushed and her black eyes were as brilliant as stars.

'You must come again,' said Yanna, kissing my cheek when she said goodbye, but although I smiled I did not answer. It wasn't very likely that I'd ever be able to come to Greece on my own and maybe I wouldn't even want to. Always, for me, the islands would be haunted by Ran's image. Especially Delos . . .

Ran and Christos escorted me back to the *Ariadne*, but then left me there. Ran explained that he wanted to treat some other Greek friends to a farewell drink at one of the local *tavernas* and warned me that the party might go on for some time.

'Shall I wait up for you?' I asked, stifling a yawn, and Ran shook his head.

'No, go to bed. I'll tell Niko and Sia to do the same.'

'All right,' I agreed. I was tired and the thought of bed was very tempting.

I undressed, washed, cleaned my teeth, brushed my hair and got into bed. The night was very still, but even so the gentle motion of the yacht was a soporific.

I was just dropping off to sleep when I heard a faint noise—a noise as though somebody was moving about in the saloon.

I was startled into immediate wakefulness. I knew that Ran couldn't possibly have returned so soon and the crew had all said goodnight and retired to their own quarters. Who, then, could possibly be in the saloon? It must be an intruder . . .

On tiptoe I was out of bed and softly opening my door. I crept noiselessly towards the saloon and caught my breath as I saw, through the partly open door, the tall figure of a broad-shouldered man, bending over as though to pick something up from the floor.

There was a large antique paperweight standing on the corner of the table. I picked it up with the vague intention of using it as a weapon if absolutely necessary and opened my mouth to scream for help.

As I did so the intruder straightened and for the first time I realised that there was something familiar about the shape of his head, the set of his shoulders. Instead of screaming I gasped, and the man spun round. One glimpse of his face, and the paperweight slipped out of my nerveless grasp and my knees threatened to buckle. It wasn't a stranger who stood facing me. It was Kit!

CHAPTER FIVE

For a moment we stood staring at each other, a moment that seemed to hang suspended for ever. Then, half laughing, half crying with surprise and relief, I almost flung myself in Kit's arms.

'Kit! Oh, Kit! How you frightened me! I never dreamt it was you! What on earth are you doing here? How did you know where to find us? Who——'

'Hey, don't be so greedy! Ask one question at a time!' Kit was laughing as he hugged me with the same casual affection with which he had greeted me all down the years. 'And where does Ran keep his brandy? I definitely need a stiff drink—for one awful moment I though you were going to brain me!'

'I though you were a b-burglar!' I explained, my voice still a bit wobbly. 'I heard a noise and as I knew Ran wasn't here and everyone else was in bed of course I was sure it was someone up to no good——'

'And instead it was just your old chum, Kit!' Kit's blue eyes laughed down at me. 'Naturally *I* thought everyone was fast asleep, so out of the kindness of my heart I tried to be as quiet as I possibly could,' He grinned. 'I know that in the past Ran and I haven't always seen eye to eye, but I must say that I certainly wasn't expecting such an—er—unfriendly reception!'

'You were just about the last person on earth I expected to see! In fact, I can still hardly believe that you're real.' I paused, then added with rising indignation, 'You've got some explaining to do, Kit Armitage! You really have!'

'I know.' Kit waited until I had found myself a chair and then perched himself on the arm, looking down into my face and smiling his familiar crooked smile.

'Do you always wear your hair in those funny little bunches nowadays?' he asked curiously, and I blushed.

'Only for bed.'

'Pity. They suit you, even if they do make you look about ten,' said Kit, contemplating me with mock-serious eyes. 'Do people take you and Tamsin for twins?'

'We're not a bit alike and Tamsin is eight, not ten. Anyway, how do you know——'

'About Tamsin's being on board? Simple, dear heart. I found a letter from Ran waiting for me when I returned to Athens, telling me that he'd invited you both to be his guests on the *Ariadne*. He also suggested that since I hadn't seen fit to come home for Easter, as I'd promised, I might like to join the party myself. He told me what islands you were visiting en route for Crete, and when, and said that wherever I turned up I'd be very welcome.'

Ignoring my gasp of surprise, Kit suddenly bent down and captured my hands. 'Annabel, did I really mess things up for you? Ran said you were fearfully disappointed when I didn't show up and more or less intimated that I was all sorts of a heel for letting you down. Honestly I didn't think you'd mind all that much if I went to Salonika instead of coming home. I was—well, I was a bit short of funds, you see, and the air fare to England costs such a hell of a lot——'

He stopped. Then reading my incredulous look correctly he added ruefully, 'Yes, I have to admit I've been over-spending . . . living far beyond my means. And of course chucking my job didn't exactly help matters.' He frowned at my startled exclamation. 'You didn't know about that? Ran seemed to have found out all about it—I'm not sure how.'

I let that pass, though remembering the telephone calls Ran had made when we reached Athens it wasn't difficult to put two and two together. 'I'm sorry about your job, Kit. I thought you said you were enjoying learning all about antiques——'

Kit shrugged. 'It was okay to begin with, but I got bored after a time. You know me, Annabel. I like change—variety——'

'I know, but—Kit, you're nearly twenty-two! You simply must make up your mind soon what you want to do and then try to stick to it——'

'Hey!' Kit's smile had vanished. 'You're not going to start preaching at me, are you, Annabel?'

'No! No, of course not!' I spoke hastily. 'It's just that if—if you haven't found yourself another job and you're short of money——'

'Not to worry. Ran's invitation came at exactly the right time. At least I've got a couple of weeks' free board and lodging to look forward to,' Kit said cheerfully, shrugging off his denim jacket and flinging it carelessly over a chair. 'Incidentally, I wonder why Ran didn't tell you that he'd been in touch with me? I suppose he wasn't sure whether I'd want to accept his proposal or not.' He laughed. 'Almost certainly he's only prepared to put up with me because of you, Annabel my love. He must have thought that you were absolutely pining for my company——'

'I wasn't!' I said indignantly.

'Well, somehow you must have given him that impression.' Kit was laughing at my confusion. 'You needn't blush, Annabel. I know perfectly well that you regard me as a brother.' His brows suddenly drew together. 'I thought Ran knew that, too. How the devil *could* either of us possibly feel romantic about each other? After all, we practically shared the same pram!'

I said nothing, but perhaps my face wore a guilty expression, for Kit looked at me with sudden horrified suspicion.

'Annabel! You don't—you aren't——?'

'Don't be a bigger fool than you can help!' I retorted, and Kit's face cleared and he drew a long breath of relief.

'Phew! Thank goodness for that!' Then, as I laughed, 'Mind you, if I didn't know you so well it might be a different story! You're rather stunning, you know, Annabel. Pity old Charles can't see you now!'

'Charles?' I stared at him.

'Don't you remember him? He came to stay with me during the summer hols, about two years ago. He fancied you like mad, but you never gave him the slightest encouragement.'

I coloured. 'Oh, him! He had much too good an opinion of himself.'

'That wasn't the only reason you cold-shouldered

him, was it?' Kit spoke teasingly. 'I always rather suspected there was someone else, only for the life of me I couldn't think who it could be. I never ever saw you making eyes at anyone in particular——'

I caught my breath. 'That was because there wasn't anyone I felt like making eyes at! I didn't want any romantic involvements——'

'Okay.' Kit spoke soothingly. 'No need to get heated, old dear.' His brows drew together. 'Nonetheless, I'd still like to know where Ran got the idea from that you and I—well, never mind. It's quite nice to know that even he can jump to false conclusions!'

I bit my lip. 'Kit, please don't make an issue of it——'

'I wasn't going to. My poor Annabel. Have you and Ran been at loggerheads ever since you left England?' Kit asked sympathetically.

'No! Of course not!' I spoke hastily. 'He's been really nice—kind——'

'My!' Kit's brows shot up. 'You do surprise me! "Nice" and "kind" aren't the adjectives that I would normally expect you to use in connection with brother Ran——'

I caught my breath. 'Don't mock me, Kit. I know I used—used not to get on too well with Ran, but——'

'But now his charms have been presented to you in an entirely different light?' Kit's blue eyes were dancing with sudden devilment. 'Well, well! You haven't gone and fallen for him, have you, Annabel?'

'As I've said once already, don't be an idiot!' I spoke sharply: Kit of all people must never know my secret. 'Ran's about the last man on earth I'd ever fall for! He simply isn't my type——'

I stopped, suddenly aware that Kit was staring over my head at the door. A dreadful premonition seized me, I spun round and saw Ran standing in the doorway, his white dinner jacket contrasting vividly with the ebony darkness of his head. His face was expressionless, but I knew there was no way he could not have heard me.

'How nice to see you, Kit,' he said politely. 'I'm glad you could make it, but sorry that I wasn't here to welcome you on board.'

Kit's eyes gleamed. 'So am I! Annabel here thought I was a burglar and nearly crowned me! I still haven't recovered from the shock!'

'I've said I'm sorry——' I protested, scarlet-cheeked, but got no further. Laughing, Kit put his arm around my shoulder and kissed my cheek.

'Darling Annabel, I forgive you!' And then, holding me a little way away from him, 'Hey, you've grown! Your head never used to reach my shoulder, did it? I remember how annoyed you used to get whenever I called you Shrimp!' He laughed. 'Though what you really hated was Ran calling you Violet Elizabeth! That used to make you go purple with fury——'

'This is hardly the time for childhood reminiscences, Kit.' Ran's voice was cool, detached. He turned to me. 'A nightcap, Annabel? No? Well, in that case if I were you I'd go back to bed. I'll look after Kit.'

'I won't need much looking after. I'm quite prepared to doss down anywhere,' Kit said cheerfully, and pulled one of my bunches.

'*Kale nichta*, then, Annabel. See you over the coffee pot—unless you'd like me to wake you up at the crack of dawn, the way I used to, and we'll go for a swim?'

I shook my head, not daring to meet Ran's eyes. 'No, thanks. I'd rather have my beauty sleep.'

'That's my girl!' Kit, looking relieved, patted my shoulder and I smiled a little wryly to myself as I made my way back to my cabin. That's just what I wasn't ... Kit's girl. But then I wasn't Ran's girl, either, and I never ever would be.

I was last in to breakfast the following morning. Kit, wearing a bright yellow short-sleeved shirt, gave me first a friendly grin and then, as his eyes slid over my blue and white sundress that showed quite a large section of bare midriff, a look of mingled surprise and appreciation spread over his face.

'I s-a-a-a-y!' He turned to Ran. 'It's incredible, isn't it? Whoever would have thought that that skinny little brat with pigtails and long legs who used to follow me around like a puppy would turn into a raving beauty one day? Even you must agree that she's quite an eyeful——'

'Indeed, but I don't think I would express myself quite so crudely.' Ran's voice was dry. 'Stop gawping, Kit, and give Annabel a cup of coffee.'

'We've got a new kind of jam this morning. It's cherry—it's lovely,' Tamsin told me as I took my seat beside her. 'Do have some, Annabel.'

'What time did you get up, Tamsin? You must have been very quiet: I didn't hear you at all.'

'I wanted to wake you up, but Ran wouldn't let

me. He said you'd had a disturbed night and I'd got to put up with him instead. We played I-Spy,' Tamsin explained.

'Annabel thought I was a burglar when I arrived last night and tried to brain me.' Kit's blue eyes twinkled at her across the table, and I sighed to myself as Tamsin immediately demanded the full story. Obviously I was not going to be allowed to forget my unfortunate blunder—though even now I didn't see what else I could have done but pick up that paperweight!

I glanced covertly at Ran, who looked this morning as if he hadn't slept too well himself. The skin was stretched more tightly over his features than usual and there were dark lines under his eyes. It had been considerate of him to prevent Tamsin from waking me up, I thought, absently stirring my coffee, especially as he had then to entertain her himself. I had good reason to know that Tamsin was at her most demanding first thing in the morning: it was only later in the day that her energy sometimes flagged a little.

She was giggling now at Kit's dramatic account of his arrival, her eyes sparkling, her small face rosy with mirth. I had wondered how she would react to Kit's presence ... whether she would resent his joining our small circle ... but evidently I needn't have worried. It seemed, I thought wryly, that small girls were just as vulnerable to Kit's charm as everyone else. Or nearly everyone else. Judging by the bleakness of Ran's face this morning, he was in no mood to be charmed by anyone.

'What time are we leaving Mykonos, Ran?' Tamsin asked, looking at him expectantly as he finished his coffee. 'Can we go ashore for a little while, please? I'd like to stretch my legs.'

'Yes, that's all right. I'm going ashore myself, but don't be too long—an hour at the most,' Ran warned her.

'I wonder if we'll see Melita,' Tamsin remarked when some twenty minutes later she, Kit and I were walking along the waterfront. Even at that hour in the morning the sun was shining brilliantly and everywhere there was noise and bustle—housewives shouting, children running in and out of doorways. 'Didn't she say she might come and wave goodbye to us, Annabel?'

'No, she didn't.' I spoke absently, my eyes on the never-ending streams of tourists as they flowed past dressed in all conceivable garments from flowing kaftans to frayed jeans. Most of them seemed to be making for the shops, though Tamsin and I both felt that we had had our fill of pottery and silverware and knick-knacks and were certainly not tempted to spend any more of our precious drachmas.

Surprisingly, Kit did not know Mykonos at all well and Tamsin was so anxious to show him as many of our favourite views as possible that we had to keep the *Ariadne* and our eleven o'clock rendezvous firmly in mind or we should have lingered in the town for hours. As it was, we were nearly ten minutes late, but since luckily Ran was late, too, it didn't really matter.

There was no sign of Melita, though both Tamsin and I kept a watchful eye on the quay. Just before half-past eleven we sailed, and I was forced to the regretful conclusion that she had been unable to face the prospect of saying goodbye to us. I hoped that one day I would see her again—perhaps when she finally attained her dearest wish and came to London.

It was a calm, bright day and the *Ariadne* glided with its customary serenity over the deep saxe-blue sea. The far promontory of Mykonos came and went in a faint, mauve-blue haze and I saw Delos lying to the north. Delos, the sacred island, the one island I would never forget. Except that I must . . .

The day wore on. I think that perhaps I must have lost all sense of time in the drowsiness of sun and sparkling blue water and the almost hypnotic drone of the engines, for it was a shock when I eventually discovered that it was late afternoon.

A fairly stiff breeze had sprung up and since I was wearing only a sleeveless shift I decided that instead of sitting on deck and feeling uncomfortably chilly I would fetch a cardigan from my cabin.

I was humming to myself as I opened the door—a gay, catchy little tune that was often on Niko's lips as he went about his work. I had no inkling, no premonition of what I should see. In fact, I didn't even notice at first that there was someone else in my cabin. I bent to pull open a drawer in my dressing table and as I did so a familiar voice spoke from behind me.

'Hello, Annabel.'

For one dazed, incredulous moment I thought I must be dreaming. Then I spun round, and saw— Melita! She was sitting on the edge of my bed and smiling, though I thought that her big eyes held a touch of apprehension as she waited for my reaction.

It was the second shock I'd had in rather less than twenty-four hours and so perhaps it was not really surprising that I simply stood and gaped at her in utter incredulity.

'Melita!' I exclaimed, and leant against the wall of the cabin, wondering just for a moment if I was suffering from hallucinations. Melita, wearing a pale blue pleated skirt, a navy jacket swinging open over a white shirt, with a blue, polka-dotted cravat knotted loosely around her throat, certainly looked substantial enough, but——

'Annabel darling, please don't be cross!' Melita's small, heart-shaped face wore an expression that was half defiant, half appealing. 'It was you who put the idea in my head—about being a stowaway, I mean! I know you were only joking, but—but I kept thinking about what fun it would be and—and in the end I couldn't help wondering if I could possibly get away with it! Quite honestly I was almost sure I'd be caught, but when I arrived this morning there wasn't anyone in sight and it was the easiest thing in the world to find a hiding place! I didn't have any trouble at all. There—there was this empty locker, you see— I was in there for *hours*! I only crept out a few minutes ago—I'd got cramp so badly that I just couldn't stand it any longer——'

'Melita!' I had been listening in a kind of daze, but now I interrupted the breathless flow of words. 'Do your parents know you're here?'

Melita's dark eyes widened with astonishment. 'Don't be *silly*, Annabel! Of course they don't! At least—well, I left them a note, and they may have found it by now, I suppose. I told them that there was nothing to worry about and that I'd get in touch with them as soon as I could. You did say Naxos was your next port of call, didn't you?'

'Unless Ran decides to turn round and take you straight back to Mykonos.' I spoke grimly. 'Melita, of all the crazy, idiotic things to do! Goodness only knows what Ran will say to you! He'll probably be absolutely furious——'

'But why?' There was a flicker of dismay in Melita's dark eyes, but she lifted her chin defiantly. 'One more passenger won't make much difference, will it, Annabel? I won't be any trouble, really I won't. I'll be company for you and I'll help to look after Tamsin and——' She stopped. Then in a small voice she said, 'I—I thought you'd be *pleased*, Annabel! You said how much you'd miss me—that you all would——'

'Oh, Melita!' I gave an unsteady laugh. 'Don't be an idiot! Of course I'm pleased to see you, but I'm not so sure about Ran. He's bound to be worried about your parents' reaction. If they're at all upset——'

'They won't be. I've explained everything in my note.' Melita spoke confidently. 'As long as Ran isn't too angry with me everything will be all right, Annabel, I'm sure it will.' She drew a deep breath. 'Where is he? Maybe I'd better go and show myself straight away.'

'He's up on deck, with Kit and Tamsin.'

Melita stopped dead in her tracks, swung round and stared at me. '*Kit?*'

'Ran's brother. He arrived last night—or, more correctly, early this morning.' I managed to smile.

'Somewhat unexpectedly, a little like you, Melita.'

'Oh, no!' Melita sat down again rather suddenly, her face the picture of dismay. 'I didn't think—I didn't know—oh, Annabel, I *am* sorry! How foolish I have been! Now I've gone and spoilt everything for you! No wonder you weren't pleased to see me. You don't need anyone else now you've got Kit, do you? I shall only be in the way. Maybe the best thing I can do is to ask Ran to take me back to Mykonos straightaway——'

'Rubbish!' Completely recovered now from my initial shock, though I was still a little anxious about Ran's reaction to the presence of a stowaway, I spoke quickly. Melita was a little wretch, but I really was fond of her and I hated to see her looking suddenly so woebegone. 'Of course you won't be in anyone's way!' I hesitated, then added a little awkwardly, 'I told you right at the beginning that I'd known Ran and Kit all my life. Kit is even more like a brother to me than—than Ran is.'

Melita looked at me. 'Is that really true, Annabel?'

'Yes, it really is, Melita. You don't have to worry one little scrap about playing gooseberry——'

'Playing gooseberry?'

Melita's bewildered expression was so comical that in spite of myself I had to laugh. She had had a British nursemaid when she was small and as a result her English was so good—and quite often so amazingly colloquial—that I sometimes forgot that it wasn't her native tongue.

'I'm sorry. It's just a saying we have in English. It means being an unwanted third when—when lovers are together.'

'Oh, I see.' Melita's eyes danced. Then she added quaintly, 'Now you have explained, Annabel, I can tell you that I am very much looking forward to meeting this Kit. From what I've heard he isn't a bit like Ran.'

'He isn't,' I said, adding—but under my breath so that Melita couldn't possibly hear me—'No one could be. Not ever.'

Ran was alone when we eventually found him. His jaw dropped when he caught sight of Melita, but he quickly recovered his self-possession and listened in grim-faced silence to her nervous confession. He was angry, just as I'd suspected he would be, but principally, he told Melita, because she had behaved very badly towards her parents.

'What I ought to do is to take you straight back to Mykonos,' he said sternly, but Melita clutched hold of his arm, her big eyes so imploring that I thought they could surely melt an iceberg.

'Oh, please, Ran! Please don't do that! I can telephone my parents from Naxos! Please wait and see what they say first!' she begged him.

Ran looked at her, his jaw a little squarer than usual. 'You're a baggage, Melita. You deserve to be spanked—or worse. Do you happen to know the classic punishment for stowaways?' he asked, sounding so severe that poor Melita, looking really apprehensive, shrank back.

Ran took a step towards her. I saw Melita's eyes widen with fear and spoke quickly.

'Ran, in a way it was my fault. I put the idea into her head, I'm afraid,' I confessed.

'I might have known it!' Suddenly Ran's lips

twitched and I saw a gleam of something that might have been humour in his dark eyes. 'Then perhaps it's you I should punish, Annabel. Let's see—what would be suitable? I can hardly cast you both into irons——'

'Why not make them both walk the plank?' suggested a laughing voice, and I looked round to see Kit standing just behind us, grinning mischievously. Obviously he had heard most of Melita's confession, for when I hurriedly introduced him he regarded her with dancing eyes that held also, I was quick to note, a glint of very obvious admiration.

'I've always wanted to meet a stowaway,' he told her solemnly, his gaze sweeping appreciatively over her delicate features and lingering on her mouth. I recognised the predatory look and also the way Melita reacted to it by unconsciously straightening and putting up a hand to pat her disordered hair. 'When we were children Annabel and I used to think it would be great fun to conceal ourselves on a ship bound for some exotic place like Casablanca or Rio de Janeiro, but we never quite had the nerve to do it.'

'I hope what you really mean is that one of you, at least, retained a modicum of common sense.' Ran spoke drily, his eyes, too, on Melita's face. It was now the colour of a wild rose and she was looking at Kit almost as though she was dazzled by what she saw. I tried to look at him through her eyes and realised, with a sense almost of shock, that some girls—especially a girl as young as Melita—might find his blond good looks even more attractive than Ran's aloof darkness.

'I'm afraid I've been rather silly,' Melita murmured, giving Kit an enchantingly rueful glance from beneath her long, gold-tipped lashes. 'Ran is quite right to be angry with me, only—only I do hope he isn't *too* angry, because I should simply hate to be sent back to Mykonos in disgrace!'

Kit and I both turned to look at Ran, whose dark brows were drawn together in a heavy frown.

'You won't take the poor kid back, will you?' Kit asked. 'At least, not unless it's what her parents say they want you to do?'

Ran hesitated almost imperceptibly. His eyes sought mine and although I don't know what he read in them he gave a brief nod.

'All right. I'll contact Yanna and Christos directly we reach Naxos. In the meantime, Miss Machelevos' —he looked at her severely—'you'd better behave yourself, or else!'

'Oh, I will! I'll be *very* good!' Melita almost blazed with delighted relief. 'I've already promised Annabel I won't be any trouble, Ran, and that I'll help to amuse Tamsin——'

'Which reminds me, where is she?' I spoke lightly, trying not to stare at Kit, who had an expression on his face I'd never seen before. If he had made a favourable impression upon Melita then she had almost bowled him over, I thought, alarmed, and made a mental note to let him know as soon as possible that for all her apparent maturity Melita was actually only seventeen.

'Let me go and find her. I'd like to surprise her,' Melita said eagerly, and Kit laughed.

'I know where she is. I left her in the galley, trying

to wheedle Sia into making her some gingerbread men. You don't know your way around the *Ariadne* yet, I suppose? Come on, I'll show you.'

I didn't attempt to follow them. Instead I looked at Ran, who was still frowning. Was he really afraid that Yanna and Christos would be upset and angry because their adored daughter had resorted to such unconventional methods in an effort to relieve her boredom? I wondered. Because I didn't think they would be. Had Melita asked their permission to accompany us to Crete I was sure they would have given it gladly. They liked me and they admired and respected Ran. Once they'd been assured that her presence on the *Ariadne* was not unwelcome, they'd probably stop worrying. So why did Ran, who knew just how much Melita was petted and indulged, look at me so oddly when I said, 'I'm glad you're willing to let her stay, Ran. You—you don't really mind having an extra passenger, do you?'

Ran hesitated. Then slowly he said, 'The funny thing is that I nearly invited her to join us. She's a nice child and I could see how much you and Tamsin liked her. I didn't do it only because——' He stopped.

'Because?'

Ran hesitated again and then he shrugged. 'Because I was half expecting Kit and I knew that if he turned up you certainly wouldn't want anyone else,' he said bluntly.

I felt my face flame. 'Ran, that's silly! Kit and I aren't—we don't want——' I stopped helplessly as I saw Ran's unbelieving smile.

'You mean you're sorry I invited him?'

'Of course not! It—I—Ran, I've been meaning to

say that I thought it was awfully nice of you. You—
you did it for me, didn't you? Because you thought I
was so disappointed about not seeing him——'

'Well, weren't you?' Ran asked coolly, but I bit my
lip.

'Yes, but——'

'But you'd rather not have been beholden to me
for Kit's favours? Is that it?' Ran sounded suddenly
angry. 'Well, as it happens you don't owe me very
much, do you? Indirectly, it seems that I may well
have done you a bad turn!'

I looked at him in bewilderment. 'A bad turn?'

Ran's mouth went down at one corner. 'Didn't you
see the way Kit looked at Melita? Or are you so sure
of your hold over him that you don't really mind if
just occasionally he gives another girl the glad eye?'
he jeered softly.

I caught my breath. 'Ran, you're a beast!'

Ran's smile was bitter. 'Which means, I suppose,
that as usual your beloved Kit can do no wrong!
Okay, Annabel. Forget it,' he said, pulling a wry face,
and with a shrug of his broad shoulders he turned
away.

Considerably shaken, I made my escape. So Ran,
too, had noticed the effect that Melita and Kit had
had on each other! And—not unnaturally—he'd
thought I might be jealous. Well, that didn't matter
too much, but for everyone's sake I'd better try to
warn Kit not to show his admiration quite so plainly
in future. If Melita was to stay with us on the *Ariadne*
and later in Crete then Ran would feel himself responsible for her well-being and he certainly wasn't

likely to approve of her becoming romantically involved with his younger brother!

Except—when Venetia arrived would he notice
anything or anyone else at all besides her? Somehow,
I didn't think it was very likely.

CHAPTER SIX

AGAINST the changing colours of sea and sky, islands came and went, some fairly large, others little more than a bare brown shoulder and a rocky point or two.

Melita, at first, seemed a little subdued, but Kit's high spirits were infectious and soon she was her usual vivacious self. Kit, I could see, continued to find her fascinating, something I wouldn't have minded at all if I hadn't felt so guilty about the way I'd led Ran to believe that my feelings for his brother were a lot stronger than they really were. Luckily, I was able to console myself with the thought that after the gentle warning I'd given Kit a casual observer would have been hard put to it to decide whose company he preferred, Melita's or mine. Unfortunately, Melita was far more transparent and I could only hope that Ran was too preoccupied with other matters to notice how suddenly she seemed to have grown up. She had been pretty before, but now she almost blazed with a beauty that contained so much maturity that even I was astonished, and when Kit was around she looked so radiantly happy that I found myself wondering why the Greeks had never had a goddess of joy.

I had a lot of sympathy with her since it was only in Ran's company that I myself ever seemed to be truly, warmly alive. That still held good even though ever since Kit and Melita had joined us there was very little intimacy between us. He was unfailingly polite, but his manner towards me was detached and impersonal and most of his attention seemed to be centred on Tamsin. I couldn't help feeling glad, for his sake, that although Kit made a big fuss of her it was still quite obviously Ran she liked best, even when he was in one of his silent, abstracted moods.

'That child thinks the world of Ran, doesn't she?' Kit remarked to me in some surprise, and I nodded, my eyes on Ran as he sat patiently trying to teach his small goddaughter to tie a fisherman's knot.

'Yes. He's very fond of her, too.'

'Hm. Things could become a little awkward later on, then,' Kit observed thoughtfully, and I turned to stare at him.

'Awkward? What do you mean?'

Kit shrugged. 'Oh, I've heard the odd rumour and it's not too difficult to put two and two together. It's common knowledge that Paul's and Venetia's marriage is heading for the rocks and it's pretty obvious, isn't it, who Venetia has got lined up as Paul's successor? I suppose she realises, now, that she ought to have married Ran in the first place, but I must say it all seems to be rather hard on Tamsin. However much she thinks of Ran she's bound to feel that she ought to side with her father——'

'Kit!' I interrupted him, my voice fierce. 'I've never heard anything so monstrous in all my life! Ran would never—he wouldn't dream of—Paul is his *friend*! He wouldn't marry Venetia, not knowing how much it would hurt Paul and Tamsin! I know he wouldn't! Not—not however much he loves her!'

Kit raised his eyebrows. 'Well, there's no need to bite my head off, dear girl! I was only expressing an opinion. However, I think you'll find that I'm right.'

I waited a moment to regain control of myself, then quietly I said, 'Well, I hope you're not, Kit. Divorce is usually a horrid, messy business and especially where children are concerned.'

Kit shrugged. 'These things do happen, unfortunately. It's no good being old-fashioned about them, Annabel.'

I had never in my life come nearer to disliking Kit than at that moment. I turned away from him, my lips tightly compressed, but luckily just at that moment Melita, who was leaning over the rail, turned her head to shout that she had sighted Naxos.

'Naxos ... that's where Theseus ran away from poor Ariadne, wasn't it? After she'd helped him slay the Minotaur, too!' Tamsin said reproachfully, abandoning her knot to join Melita at the rail.

The story of the Princess Ariadne was fresh in my mind, too, but there seemed to be very little about Naxia, the island's harbour town, to link it with that most attractive of all Greek heroines and I was quite glad when Ran decided that we would only pay it a fleeting visit. Kit and Tamsin and I wandered for a little while through the narrow streets and then sat and sipped cool drinks on the waterfront while Ran and Melita went off to make a telephone call to Yanna and Christos which, luckily, eventually resulted in smiles all round.

That little bit of business having been disposed of, we left Naxia and sailed round the island, the largest and most fertile of the whole Cyclades group, until

we found an attractive little inlet at the southern
end. Here we anchored for a bathe and lunch on a
lonely beach which, Ran solemnly assured a wide-
eyed Tamsin, was quite probably the very one on
which Theseus had so callously abandoned his beautiful princess.

After lunch Ran and Kit and Melita and I lay on
our towels on the hot sand while Tamsin wandered
about looking for shells and pretty pebbles which she
put into a gaily coloured raffia bag that Sia had given
her. After a time Ran got up to help her and a few
minutes later Melita suggested going for another
swim.

I shook my head. 'Count me out. I'm feeling lazy.
But you and Kit go if you want to, Melita.'

'Sure you don't mind?' Melita was all eagerness
and so was Kit. Hand-in-hand they ran down to the
water, but before they plunged in they both turned
to me and waved and laughed and I waved back.
Suddenly I thought how lucky Melita was. She seemed
not to be afflicted by any of the usual problems of
adolescence and her self-confidence was amazing.
Maybe, if I'd been like that at her age——

I sighed, and sitting up ran a comb through my
tangled hair. It was only when I'd been swimming
that I wished it was shorter: usually I liked the feel
of its warm silky weight on my shoulders.

I folded my towel beneath my head and lay down
again on the warm sand. I felt pleasantly drowsy and
perhaps I dozed off, for when I next opened my eyes
I saw, emerging from the distant golden haze, a
slender girl, who wore a long, flowing dress which
moulded her figure in the seductive way of a Greek

statue and who carried her dark head as proudly as a princess. *Ariadne*, I thought stupidly. For a moment my mouth went dry, then I smiled at myself for my folly. It was a flesh-and-blood girl and not a wraith I saw ... a girl who was calling a flock of about fifty goats after her and whose dignified, almost regal carriage was undoubtedly the graceful legacy of a lifetime of carrying pots of water balanced on her head.

I delved in my beach bag for my sunglasses and when I again looked up it was to see Ran walking towards me, his wide shoulders outlined against the sun.

'You've been asleep.'

I shook my head. 'Not really. I think I dozed, though, just for a moment.' I grinned ruefully. 'I almost thought I saw poor Ariadne's ghost.'

Ran sat down beside me. 'Ghosts don't walk in the sunshine, Annabel. And in any case, why "poor" Ariadne?'

'Isn't it obvious? Her lover deserted her——'

'But she found happiness with Dionysus. According to the legend she bore him many children, and the whole of nature burst into bloom to share their happiness. Dionysus even hung a necklace of stars in the sky for his princess—the Corona Borealis.'

'He must have loved her very much——'

'Yes. So she isn't really to be pitied, is she?'

I shook my head without speaking and watched as Ran picked up a handful of fine white sand and let it shift through his fingers. Abruptly, without looking at me, he said, 'Why don't you join Kit and Melita? They seem to be enjoying themselves.'

I followed the direction of his gaze. Melita and Kit were fooling around in the shallows, throwing cas-

cades of water at each other, bathed in sunlight ...
golden boy and golden girl.

'I don't feel energetic enough. Perhaps I ate too
much lunch. That heavenly *salata*——'

'You ate scarcely anything. I was watching you.'

'Oh.' I was taken aback, immediately on the defen-
sive. 'Why?'

Now Ran was tracing patterns on the sand with a
lean brown finger. 'Shall we just say that I feel ...
responsible ... for your welfare?'

Somehow that annoyed me. 'You needn't worry!
I'm perfectly all right!' I snapped.

'Are you?' Ran rolled over and looked at me and
at something I saw in his face—an utterly unexpected concern—I caught my breath. I wanted so
much to move into his arms so that I had to close my
eyes so that he shouldn't see the way I felt. 'You
really are perfectly happy, Annabel? Even though
Kit——'

'Even though Kit what?' I asked breathlessly. 'I'm
not jealous of Melita, if that's what you're driving at,
Ran.'

His eyes narrowed. 'I'll accept that statement—
from you, though God knows most women *would* be
jealous, given a similar situation. Which poses an interesting question. *Why* aren't you jealous? Either
you have unbounded faith in Kit's loyalty and your
own attractions, or else——'

'Or else?' I spoke shakily, my hands pressing down
hard to either side of me on the warm sand.

'Or else you're not really in love with Kit at all.
But if you aren't—if you're not jealous of the attention he's paying to Melita—why such sad eyes, such

a bleak little face? You weren't like this before.'

I wanted to say, 'No. But before I wasn't really worried about you and Venetia, and now I am. Because if anyone gets hurt it's going to be Tamsin and it's not fair, when she's such a darling ...' but of course I didn't. I remained silent.

'Well?' Ran asked softly, his eyes probing my face.

I began to mumble an excuse, but mercifully just then the sound of animated voices cut through our solitude. Kit and Melita were returning from their swim, with Tamsin trailing behind them.

'That was wonderful!' Melita flung himself down beside me and sat with her bronzed arms round her knees, her curly dark hair glistening in the sun and her skin glowing. Everything about her had a bloom of health and youth. 'You ought to have come with us, Annabel.'

'I'm not a mermaid like you.' I smiled at Kit, weak with relief at having been spared a further inquisition. 'I sometimes think that water is Melita's natural element.'

'She's certainly very good,' Kit agreed admiringly, and Melita laughed.

'Not nearly as good as you! Do you scuba-dive, Kit?'

Kit's face lit up. 'Rather! I love it. What about you?'

'I love it, too. Of course, the conditions are ideal here—the water's so clear. I keep hoping I'll find something really valuable one day.'

'A sunken treasure ship?' I teased.

'Oh, at the very least,' Melita agreed. 'Or maybe a temple or two—relics of lost Atlantis——'

'Atlantis never existed,' Ran told her, and Melita opened her eyes wide.

'Oh, but it did! And probably somewhere quite near here, too—at any rate in the Aegean Sea! Isn't that right, Annabel?'

I remembered a book I had once read. 'Poseidon lived in Atlantis with Cleito, his beloved, and they had ten sons, five sets of twins,' I said dreamily. 'The roofs of the houses were of red copper, which shone in the sun, and there were two gorgeous temples, one of which had silver walls, golden pinnacles and a roof of ivory, copper, gold and silver.'

Ran was laughing. 'Annabel, Annabel! Didn't I tell you you were a romantic?'

'I don't care. I *want* to believe in Atlantis,' I said defiantly.

'So do I,' said Melita. 'Along with flying saucers and the Bermuda Triangle——'

Kit laughed. 'And werewolves and vampires——'

'Piskies and fairy rings. Oh, and Father Christmas, of course. We mustn't forget him.' That was Tamsin's enthusiastic contribution. She looked at me. 'What else, Annabel?'

'What about happy endings? Maybe you even believe in those, too,' said Ran, so cynically that I couldn't think of anything to say. I certainly couldn't protest. He must know, as I knew, that there could be no happy ending as far as he and Paul and Venetia were concerned. At least, not a happy ending for all three.

Mid-afternoon we reluctantly abandoned our secluded beach and made our way back to Naxia. We were still anchored there when much to our concern we found that Sia was unwell. Ran noticed at dinner that her face was pale and drawn and when questioned she reluctantly admitted that she was suffering from some kind of a stomach upset. She tried to make light of her symptoms, but not surprisingly Ran insisted upon her going to bed and staying there until she felt better.

'We shall probably have to buckle to and prepare our own meals tomorrow,' he told us. 'Melita, can you cook?' Then, as she shook her head, 'Annabel?'

'Of course.' I answered him promptly, though caution made me add, 'As long as you don't expect anything too elaborate——'

'Well, we won't expect Cordon Bleu dishes, that's for sure,' said Ran, a flicker of amusement in his dark eyes. 'And of course we'll all help as much as we can. Kit and I can toast bread, if nothing else.'

'Thanks, but I'd far rather have the galley to myself. I couldn't possibly exercise my—er—talents with two hefty blokes getting under my feet,' I said firmly. 'You can keep out, all of you,' And then, seeing the disappointment on Tamsin's face, 'One exception. Tamsin.'

'I can't cook, you know,' Tamsin said wistfully. 'I asked Venetia once if she'd teach me, but she never has.'

It was on the tip of my tongue to say that I couldn't imagine glamorous, exotic Venetia doing anything quite so mundane as peeling potatoes or frying bacon, but I bit the words back just in time.

'Cooking's mostly common sense, and you've got quite a lot of that,' I told her. 'A good cookery book comes in useful, too.' I paused, then added ruefully, 'I don't suppose Sia's will be much use to me, though.'

In actual fact I was quite looking forward to step-ping into Sia's shoes for a day or two. I rather felt that I would enjoy the challenge of producing palatable meals from the kind of ingredients that probably wouldn't be found in most English kitchens. I might even, I thought to myself, be able to surprise Ran. I had a feeling that he did not think of me as being in the least domesticated, but my mother was not a North-Country woman for nothing and though as a small girl I had preferred an outdoor life to anything else she had still insisted on teaching me how to cook and sew.

I was in bed when I suddenly realised that if I had to prepare breakfast for a number of people it might be quite a good idea to find out beforehand what food was in stock and plan a menu accordingly. Melita, in the twin bed next to mine, was already fast asleep and I thought that Kit and Ran had also retired to their cabins, but I was wrong. Much to my mortifica-tion, since I hadn't even bothered to put on my slip-pers, I bumped into Ran just as he was emerging from the saloon.

His eyebrows shot up and he looked amused when I explained my errand.

'The freezer is well stocked, so we shan't starve whatever happens,' he assured me. 'You can stop worrying and go back to bed.' He hesitated. 'Unless you'd like to go up on deck for a breath of fresh air? That's where I'm going.'

'Oh, I don't think——' I began hesitantly, but Ran didn't let me finish. He took hold of my arm.

'Come and have a look at the stars. It's a superb night—the visibility's perfect.'

My heart suddenly racing, I followed him up to the top deck. The night, as he'd said, was unbelievably beautiful with the sky a deep, velvety blue-black and thousands of stars coruscating with a diamond-like brilliance. The yacht's brasses gleamed in the moonlight and phosphorus was iridescent in the water.

'British astronomers would give a fortune for skies like these!' Ran remarked. 'Good observing conditions are a rarity in our part of the northern hemisphere, unfortunately. There's nearly always too much cloud.'

As we leant over the rail his arm brushed against mine and once again I was conscious of the old dangerous magic stirring my blood and quickening my senses. When I spoke, however, my voice sounded cool and matter-of-fact.

'Is that why we're building a new observatory somewhere abroad? I seem to remember reading something about it in the newspapers.'

'Yes. Britain and Spain have agreed to co-operate in building a Northern Hemisphere observatory on the island of Las Palmas in the Canary Islands. I've seen the selected site—the peak of Fuente Nueva— and since several solar telescopes will eventually be installed there, forming an international solar observatory, the possibilities are truly tremendous. There's no reason why Las Palmas shouldn't become the centre of a unique international co-operation, with Britain's giant optical telescopes dominating the whole scene.'

'Will you be involved, do you think?'

'I very much hope so, but of course a lot depends.'

'On what?' I asked curiously, and Ran grinned.

'On several factors. For instance, I may marry and find that my wife doesn't relish the idea of living half-way up a mountain.'

I felt hollow inside. He didn't mean Venetia . . . did he? I wanted to say, 'I'd live anywhere in the world if it meant being with you,' but instead I said with would-be casualness, 'You wouldn't ever sell Armitage Hall, would you?'

'No, I wouldn't. Kit wouldn't mind if I did, he's already told me so, but it's out of the question.' Ran spoke emphatically. 'I may not be able to spend as much time there as I'd like, but it's still home.'

'I'm glad you feel like that,' I told him, and it was true. I was glad for many reasons. I knew that the Hall dated back to Tudor times, though the Armitage family went back even further than that. The house had actually been built around the remains of an ancient keep which, before a fire in the reign of Queen Elizabeth I, had had a stirring history and one that I, proud of my North-Country heritage, knew by heart.

My people had always been farmers, but Ran and Kit came from a line of fierce, proud Border lords who had had an eye for plunder and a hard fist for holding it. Not only had they skirmished endlessly with the Scots but they had also indulged in so many private wars and bloody feuds that I'd once heard Ran say somewhat wryly that it was best not to enquire just when or why the Armitages had fought or for what, since almost certainly their dark deeds had equalled their bright.

Ran was looking at me somewhat quizzically. 'You've always loved the old place, haven't you? I can remember my father saying that you knew more about its history than either Kit or myself.'

I laughed. 'The past fascinates me. I nearly decided to read History at university instead of Modern Languages.'

'Physics and mathematics never held any charm for you, did they?'

'No. But I think perhaps I might have been interested in astronomy, if that had been on the curriculum.'

Ran smiled. 'Is that a gentle reminder that I brought you up here to show you the stars? Well, tell me where you want to start. As you can see, there are a great many set out for Madame's approval!'

Suddenly, it seemed, the hardness of his face had melted and he looked young and his eyes gay, giving him an unexpected resemblance to Kit. Was the other a mask? I wondered, confused. Was this the real Ran? Or were they both the man I loved so much? The Ran I'd never really had a chance to get to know?

A little shakily I said, 'Well, I know the names of most of the major constellations, of course, but I'm not sure that I can find them in the sky. Where are the Pleiades?'

'Over there . . . that little group of seven. In actual fact they're an open cluster of many stars—at least several hundred—but only those seven are visible to the unaided eye. To count them is a test of good eyesight,' Ran told me.

'Well, I can see them all right, so there's nothing

wrong with *my* eyes! They're beautiful, aren't they? According to the myths, don't they represent the seven daughters of Atlas, the giant who supported the world on his shoulders?'

'Right. Do you know the legend about them? They were pursued across the mountains of Boeotia by the hunter Orion and were about to fall into his clutches when they cried to Zeus for help. He took pity on them, turned them into doves and placed them in the sky.'

I laughed. 'I must remember to tell Tamsin that story. She's fascinated by all the Greek gods and goddesses.'

'They were very necessary to primitive people,' Ran pointed out. 'They desperately needed something to explain natural happenings and they found it a real comfort to think of a volcano, for instance, as a chained giant or monster or a storm at sea as an indication to Poseidon's anger. Anything that ever happened to them was the will of the gods, be it bad luck or good luck, and if they fell out with one deity —well, there was always the hope that another would come to their assistance!'

'I suppose it must have been comforting in a weird sort of way!—Where's Scorpio, Ran?'

'You can't see it at the moment. When it is in the sky its fishhook shape makes it very easy to identify, though,' Ran told me. His dark head was so close to mine that I could smell the fragrance of his tangy after-shave and I could see a tiny muscle stirring in his cheek. What had that astrologer said about those born under the sign of Scorpio? I thought wildly. 'Secret and enigmatic ... intense and passionate ...

they hold their feelings inside their hearts and rarely show their real emotions.'

'Annabel?' As if surprised by my silence Ran turned his head. Our eyes met and in his there leapt, for an instant, a light which made me catch my breath, remembering Delos. To cover my confusion I said the first thing that came into my head.

'Ran, I've been meaning to remind you ... it's Tamsin's birthday next week. We'll be at the villa by then, of course, but will——will Venetia be there? You haven't said when she'll be arriving.'

'That's because I don't really know.' Ran spoke shortly. 'The only thing I *am* certain about is that she won't be in time to help Tamsin celebrate her birthday. I'm sorry about it and so is she, but apparently it can't be helped.'

I bit my lip. 'Are you quite sure? That she won't be here in time, I mean? Tamsin is going to be horribly disappointed.'

'She's old enough to understand about career commitments,' said Ran, so curtly that I felt myself flush angrily.

'For heaven's sake! She's only eight! At that age she's entitled to hope that her mother and father will be somewhere around when she's celebrating something as important as a birthday! She's been disappointed enough as it is——'

Ran looked at me. 'Disappointed? What do you mean?'

'I mean that she expected to have a real home when her father and Venetia got married and it's never materialised!' I spoke jerkily, well aware that I was treading on dangerous ground. 'Her father's abroad half the time and Venetia is busy modelling——'

'Are you suggesting that Venetia should give up her career to become a *hausfrau*?'

I swallowed nervously. I had said too much: I could tell by the chill that had crept into his tones. 'Well, that was the original idea, wasn't it?' I asked defensively.

There was a little silence. Then Ran, his face scrupulously blank, said 'I'm sorry, Annabel. I'd really rather not discuss Venetia with you. It's too easy, at this time of night and in these circumstances, to say things that ought not to be said. I'll simply tell you this. Venetia has a problem which is causing her a great deal of heartache. Working gives her a welcome respite from that heartache. So——'

He left his sentence unfinished. There was another silence while I stared miserably at the mysterious silhouette of the sleeping island, and then he suggested, in an impersonal sounding voice, that it was time for bed.

I didn't argue. For me the moonlit night had lost its magic: even the brilliant stars had dimmed. Because Ran didn't have to tell me the cause of Venetia's heartache. I already knew.

CHAPTER SEVEN

SINCE Sia's indisposition did not last very long I didn't
have any difficulty with meals—in fact, just as I'd
suspected, I rather enjoyed my stint in the galley.
We breakfasted on fruit juice, creamy butter, deli-
cately-flavoured honey and crisp little rolls scattered
with poppy seeds, and for lunch I managed to pro-
duce *dolmades*—vine leaves stuffed with minced raw
meat and herb-seasoned rice—that were, Kit assured
me, worthy of Sia herself.

'I never realised you could cook so well. Some man
is going to acquire a treasure when he marries you!'
he said, his blue eyes laughing at me across the table,
and I saw Ran's head jerk up and the look of puzzlement on his face. To my furious embarrassment I
found myself blushing vividly. I couldn't help realising that Ran was frankly bewildered by the relationship between Kit and myself and I knew it was my
own fault entirely. Deeply, now, I regretted the way
I had tried to use Kit as a shield. It had been a bad
mistake, but of course I hadn't known then that Ran
had invited him to join us.

By the time Sia was on her feet again we had
arrived at Ios, the tiny, jewel-like island where,
according to legend, Homer had gone to die. I thought
that if the legend were really true Ios was a fitting
burial place for the great poet, for everywhere was
green and beautiful and the charm of its quiet glens,

its vineyards and little white churches, and its profusion of brightly coloured wild flowers captivated us all.

'I think that perhaps this is my favourite Greek island,' Ran told me as we stood in the square of the high town with whitewashed houses rising above us in criss-crossing streets and steps. 'Luckily it's not yet been caught in the flood of tourism—the last time I was here there weren't even any souvenir shops! And although there are seven churches in the town, there's only one disco!'

'We'll pay that a visit tonight,' Kit said with a grin, and Melita's black eyes sparkled.

'Oh yes! That would be lovely! Wouldn't it, Annabel?'

Instinctively I looked at Ran, who hesitated and then laughed.

'All right, it's a date. As Sia is better we can leave Tamsin with her: I think she's a little young to appreciate a disco!'

Rather to my surprise Tamsin didn't argue. In fact, she seemed a little subdued and once or twice during our exploration of the island I noticed that she was dragging her feet and that she was showing less than her customary enthusiasm for sightseeing.

'Don't you like Ios, Tamsin?' I asked, putting my arm round her shoulders, and she looked up at me rather pathetically.

'I feel a bit funny, Annabel. Do—do you think I could go back to the *Ariadne*? I think I'd quite like to lie down.'

'Darling, of course!' I exclaimed, angry with myself for not having noticed before how pale she was and how heavy her eyes looked. 'Have you got a headache? Do you feel sick?'

'A bit sick,' Tamsin admitted reluctantly. 'Perhaps I've got Sia's bug. It's jumped from her to me.'

I checked an involuntary laugh. 'Perhaps you have,' I agreed. 'I think you're right and the best place for you is bed, Tamsin.'

Tamsin's lips quivered. 'Yes, but I don't feel sleepy, just sick, and it's awfully lonely in bed——'

'I'll come with you, of course.' I spoke quickly and was rewarded by the blaze of relief in Tamsin's big eyes.

'Oh, Annabel, would you really? It doesn't seem fair, when you like this island so much! And there's the disco, you'll miss that, too——'

I bent and whispered in her ear. 'Don't tell anyone, but I don't like discos very much. I'd much rather stay with you.'

'Is that really necessary? For you to stay with her, I mean?' Kit protested when I explained that as Tamsin wasn't feeling very well we were both going to the *Ariadne*. 'Surely Sia can be trusted to look after her?'

'Just at the moment she'd rather have me,' I told him. 'I don't mind missing the disco, Kit.'

Ran was frowning. I guessed that he wasn't too keen on the disco, either, but that he probably felt reluctant to leave Melita alone with Kit. So far they had been reasonably circumspect, but Ran was far too observant not to have noticed that Melita's eyes followed Kit wherever he went and that Kit was by no means impervious to her charms, however much he pretended otherwise.

'Well . . . all right,' he said after a moment. 'At any rate we'll make sure we aren't too late back, Annabel.' He touched Tamsin's hair lightly. 'You should have said before that you weren't feeling very well, poppet.'

'I was all right when we landed,' Tamsin said a little tearfully. 'My tummy only started to wobble a little while ago.'

'Well, it can wobble all it likes when you're in bed,' I said cheerfully. 'I'll read you a story when you're safely tucked up. Would you like that?'

Tamsin nodded eagerly. 'Oh yes, please! Would you read me a chapter of *The Hobbit*?'

'I'll think about it,' I said, laughing. Tamsin had found a copy of *The Hobbit* among the various books I had brought with me and now the adventures of Bilbo and his friends had even taken precedence over the myths and legends of ancient Greece.

'I am so sorry! The poor little one!' Sia exclaimed, looking distressed when she saw Tamsin and myself returning to the *Ariadne* long before we were expected. 'But the sickness . . . it will not last long, I think. I was not very badly ill, it was only the *kyrios* who insisted that I should stay in bed and thus cause you extra work, *kyria*.'

'Oh, don't worry! I enjoyed myself, Sia,' I said, smiling, and then turned to Tamsin.

'Right! A lick-and-a-promise wash and then under the sheet for you, my lady!'

'I think I'm going to be sick first,' Tamsin said in a small voice, and a few moments later she was, very sick indeed. At least afterwards she felt a little more comfortable, though despite her protestations she was so tired that when I finally got her into bed she fell asleep before I'd been reading to her for more than a few minutes.

I stood looking down at her pale little face on the pillow. She looked so vulnerable ... so defenceless. A wave of indignation washed over me as I thought of the casual way in which both her father and Venetia seemed to treat her. If I had children, I thought savagely, I wouldn't be as indifferent to their feelings as Paul and Venetia seemed to be to Tamsin's. Above all else I'd try to give them security and a stable background.

I sighed as I bent to pull the thin cotton sheet over Tamsin's small, sun-browned body. Only a short time ago I'd had a dream family ... but the boys had never been fair-haired and blue-eyed, like me. However hard I'd tried to imagine them otherwise, they'd always turned out to have dark hair and eyes and a cleft in their chins, just like Ran ...

After leaving Tamsin I took some writing paper and envelopes into the saloon and settled down to write to my mother. I didn't expect to see Ran and Kit and Melita back until well after ten o'clock and I was considerably surprised to hear their voices just as I was completing my letter.

'Wasn't the disco any good?' I asked as Ran came into the saloon, closely followed by Kit and Melita, and then could have bitten out my tongue. Ran was tight-lipped, Kit's face wore a sullen expression that I knew well, and Melita looked distinctly unhappy.

It was Kit who answered me. 'I suppose it was okay, as discos go,' he said curtly. 'Want a nightcap, Melita?'

She shook her head. 'No, thanks. I—I've got rather a headache. I think I'd like to go to bed. Goodnight, everyone.'

There was a little silence after she'd left. Then Ran looked at me.

'How's Tamsin, Annabel?'

'She's all right, I think. She was sick, but she's been peacefully asleep for quite a long time now and I think she may well feel a lot better when she wakes up,' I told him.

'Good. I'll just go and take a look at her,' said Ran, and disappeared.

I drew a long breath. 'Well! What *is* the matter with everyone? What went wrong?'

'It was my fault,' Kit said gloomily. 'I got a bit carried away—well, you know what Greek bouzouki music is like and the wine we had was pretty potent, too!—and took Melita outside to—er—cool off a bit. Unfortunately, Ran had the same idea and saw me kissing her——'

'Oh *no*!' I looked at Kit in dismay. 'Kit, that was *stupid*!'

'Don't I know it!' Kit spoke ruefully. 'But I wasn't philandering, Annabel, I swear it.' He paused, colouring a little. 'Would you believe me if I told you that for the first time in my life I've fallen in love ... really in love?'

I stared at him. 'With Melita? But—Kit! You've only just met her——'

Kit shrugged. ' "Whoever loved that loved not at first sight",' he quoted.

'Good heavens!' I said feebly. And then, playing for time, 'I didn't know that you and Shakespeare were so intimately acquainted!'

'Ah! I have hidden depths, you see,' Kit spoke banteringly, then immediately sobered. 'I've been out with lots of girls. You know I have, Annabel. I've even told you about some of 'em. But Melita is the only one I've ever been sure I'd like to marry.'

I found it hard to hide my dismay. 'But Kit, you've got no job . . . no money! And Melita is only seventeen!'

Kit stuck out his chin. 'I'll find a job and stick to it, this time. As for Melita's only being seventeen—well, some girls get married when they're even younger than that!'

'Yes. Well, I advise you to tread carefully.' I spoke grimly. 'Melita is Ran's responsibility at the moment. The last thing he's likely to approve of is some kind of Romeo and Juliet affair——'

Kit's eyes glinted with reluctant laughter. 'How little you know *your* Shakespeare, Annabel my love! There's absolutely no resemblance between Melita and me and Shakespeare's ill-fated lovers! To start with, Melita's years older than Juliet was!'

'You know quite well what I meant!'

'Yes, I do.' Kit stuck his hands into the pockets of his slacks. 'The trouble is you're right, Annabel—or very nearly right. Melita went off to powder her nose——'

'Or repair the damages?'

'If you like. Anyway, that left Ran and me alone together for a few minutes and oh boy, did he tear my character to shreds!' He gave a short laugh. 'The wonder is that I've got any self-respect left, the things he said about me! It was all so crazy, too. He seemed to think that I was two-timing you—accused me of being fickle and brutal and insensitive and more or less suggested that I was going the right way about breaking your heart——'

I groaned. 'Oh, Kit! What did you say? Did you tell him that you'd fallen in love with Melita?'

Kit gave me a rueful grin. 'I don't think so. I was so hopping mad that all I said was that I didn't care what he thought of me and that I'd be immensely obliged if he'd mind his own ruddy business! Then Melita came back and we both shut up but—oh lord, Annabel, I *have* gone and made a mess of things, haven't I? Because I wouldn't put it past Ran to send me packing! If he thinks that I'm trying to seduce Melita and that I'm making you unhappy into the bargain——!'

I bit my lip but said nothing and after a moment Kit flung himself into a chair.

'I've been thinking, Annabel. Goodness only knows how or why, but Ran seems to have got hold of the idea that you're cherishing a grand passion for me, and that in the past I've—er—encouraged your feelings. Do you think that if we suddenly started acting like two little lovebirds Ran might forget he saw me kissing Melita—or else put it down to the fact that it was a beautiful moonlit night and you weren't available and she was?'

'No!' I spoke sharply, so sharply that Kit looked at me in surprise. Flushing, I said, 'I don't see how we can possibly act a lie and get away with it, Kit. Ran would know we were only pretending. He's not stupid.'

Kit shook his head. 'I think it would work, but of

course, if you're unwilling . . .' He sounded amused.

'Yes, I am. The situation is quite involved enough as it is,' I told him. 'You'll just have to be patient—I mean, where Melita is concerned. You mustn't try to rush things. And take good care you don't get carried away again by a moonlit night——'

Kit grinned. 'Don't sound so censorious! Haven't you ever let moonlight and wine and roses go to *your* head, little Miss Prunes and Prisms?'

Delos . . . the croaking of the frogs . . . the moonlight silvering ancient stones . . . the soft shiver of the sea . . . Ran's arms around me, sure and strong, his lips on mine . . .

'What's the matter? You've gone as white as a ghost!' Kit was looking at me curiously and somehow I managed to smile.

'If ever I have been carried away, Kit, I've regretted it . . . just as you have. But I've no intention of repeating my mistakes and you'd better see to it that you don't, either.'

'Think I've got less sense than you've got?' Kit retorted indignantly, and I sighed to myself. Yes, that was just what I *did* think . . . and I could see trouble ahead. On all sides. . . .

The next day, as I'd predicted, Tamsin felt so much better that she was able to enjoy her first sight of Santorin, the fabled volcanic island where the multi-coloured cliffs stoop down sheer to the sea and the best way to reach the capital, Thera, perched more than eight hundred steps up the cliffside, is by mule.

Tamsin begged to be allowed to make the ascent with us and after a moment's hesitation and an en-

quiring glance in my direction Ran agreed. I was glad
that he did, for it was an unforgettable experience,
going up a seemingly endless staircase into the sky
... a staircase with many hair-raising bends from
which we found ourselves gazing down into the turquoise sea, many feet below.

In actual fact, interesting and unusual though it
was, I didn't enjoy Santorin very much. I was still too
worried about the altercation between Ran and Kit
and its possible repercussions. Ran had said nothing
to me about the incident, but he was cool towards Kit
and there was noticeable constraint between Kit and
Melita. I had half expected the latter to confide in me,
but she hadn't, possibly, I thought wryly, because in
spite of my assurances she still believed I might be in
love with Kit.

After Santorin, Crete, Homer's 'fair and fertile land
out in the midst of the wine-dark deep', was our last
port of call. Here we had to say goodbye to the
Ariadne and her crew, our sadness mitigated by our
appreciation of the rugged beauty of the island and
our anticipation of what must come next.

'Is the villa very big? Has it got a garden?' Tamsin
demanded excitedly as Ran and Kit loaded our baggage into the boot of an ancient taxi, and Ran
laughed.

'Wait and see!' he teased. 'We'll be there soon.'

We left the harbour, with its hawk-faced fishermen
and women wearing shawls and black kirtles, its
rainbow-coloured caiques bobbing about on the water
and its mingled scents of retsina, ouzo, pine dust and
fish, behind us and began climbing a narrow dusty
road which rose in steep, hairpin bends for a con-

siderable distance. We were travelling inland so that the scenery consisted mainly of tree-clad hills and lower hills and foothills and orange and olive groves, but occasionally we caught a glimpse of the sapphire-blue sea and I was conscious all the time of the sweet dusty smell of fig leaves and the more aromatic scents of other small hardy plants—rosemary, lavender and wild thyme.

Tamsin sat clutching my hand, wide-eyed with excitement. We passed through some pine woods and groves of olive trees and then, a few minutes later, through a small village where the houses were washed ochre and pink and dazzling white, with rose-red roofs and flowering plants festooning walls and balconies. There seemed to be no men about but I saw several black-shawled women with panniered donkeys and some scantily dressed children, playing in the dust, who waved to us in a friendly fashion as we passed.

'Not far to go now,' Ran observed, and indeed the Villa Samphira was just around the next bend ... I recognised it from the photographs that Ran had shown me. It was set back from the road in a luxuriant garden full of roses, geraniums and canna lilies, it had whitewashed walls and green shutters and, at the back, I glimpsed an orchard of lemon and orange trees which fell away to a sheet of glittering blue lurex that was the sea.

A very old woman in a black dress and a white apron came out to welcome us, and a young man appeared from nowhere and began to haul out our luggage. Tamsin and Melita and I stood on the path at the bottom of a flight of stone steps, aware of blazing sunlight and sleepy silence and hot, sweet scents, and then followed Ran and Kit through a cream-painted door into the villa's shadowy interior. The hall with its mosaic floor and sage-hued walls was fragrant with the scent of roses: a huge urn of vivid pink ones, full-blown and hot with sun, stood on a pedestal at the foot of a shallow staircase.

The old woman, whose name was Sofia, showed me into a pretty blue and white bedroom. Tamsin had a little room next door and Melita had a larger room at the end of a corridor, overlooking the sea.

'Doesn't it seem funny to be in a house again?' said Tamsin, giggling. 'I keep expecting the floor to go up and down!'

I went to the window, pushing back the shutters which had been partly closed against the glare of the sun.

'It's rather nice to look out of a window and see flowers and trees instead of nothing but sea, Tamsin.'

She danced over to my side. 'I'm going to like it here. Aren't you?'

'I expect so.' I smiled at her. 'Won't you miss Sia?'

'A little, but I've still got you and Venetia will be here next week.' Tamsin's face was alight with happy anticipation. 'I wish she was going to be in time for my birthday, but Ran says I can have a party, if I like, and he's going to give me a very, very special present.'

How like Ran, I thought, to remember what I'd told him about Tamsin's disappointment and to try to make amends. Aloud I said, 'And I'll make you a birthday cake.'

Tamsin's eyes sparkled. 'With icing? And candles?'

'Icing, of course, and candles if I can get them. I'll write your name on top of the cake and decorate it with roses,' I said recklessly.

'Darling Annabel!' Tamsin flung her arms around my neck. 'Oh, I do love you! You're so terribly nice!'

'Cupboard love!' I teased. 'Go and wash your face! You've been eating peaches: your mouth's all sticky.'

Tamsin pulled a face at me but did as she was told. I, too, had a quick wash and then began to rummage in one of my suitcases for a clean dress. The one I found was white, and I realised as I put it on how well it showed off my sun-browned legs and arms.

I was putting a few things away when there was a knock at the door and I saw Melita standing there, wearing a flame-coloured dress that enhanced her vivid colouring.

'Isn't it lovely, Annabel? There's even a little private beach: my bedroom overlooks it.'

'Super,' I agreed, and after collecting Tamsin we went downstairs to explore our new surroundings.

Ran was nowhere to be seen, but Kit was already waiting for us, anxious to point out the path that led through the garden and down on to the beach. There wasn't very much of it, but the sand was dazzlingly white and there were ice-daisies, pink and crimson, splashing down over sunlit rock and the dappled dimness of a grove of pine trees afforded some welcome shade.

Melita, with Kit beside her, was looking happy again but evidently he had found an opportunity to warn her that in front of Ran, at least, they must hide their feelings for each other, for at dinner she scarcely glanced in his direction and gave most of her attention to Tamsin.

I was glad that we were eating outside. The sky was again thick with stars and flickering candles made little pools of radiance on the tiled floor of the small, enclosed patio. All around were flowering vines whose scent pierced sweetly through the velvet darkness and I thought how lucky I was, to be eating wonderful Greek food and drinking *ouzo* in the deep, soft blue of a southern night. So why wasn't I happier? Then I looked up and saw Ran staring into space, and his thoughts were so obviously far away with Venetia that the little jealous ache in my heart supplied the answer to my question.

If it hadn't been for that odd little ache, and my constant fear that if Ran discovered that Kit was really serious about Melita there might be unpleasant consequences, the next few days would have been utterly perfect. The sun continued to shine from a cloudless blue sky and we all spent a lot of time either splashing about in the sea or lying on the beach in the white blaze of the sun.

We also, of course, did quite a lot of exploring. There were two cars at the villa and with these at our disposal the island slowly became familiar. It was a land of contrasts, of oil and garlic and fruit hot and sweet from trees, and I felt I should never tire of its snow-capped mountains striking fiercely into the astonishing sky, its splendid remains of past civilisations, its tiny villages, whitewashed and full of shadows and quiet, still heat, its silver olive groves and its little harbours with red and green and blue caiques swinging gently at their moorings.

Tamsin was now perfectly fit again and becoming increasingly excited about her approaching birthday. I had bought her a present—a really beautiful Greek doll—and Sofia had allowed me to bake her a cake, but neither Melita nor Kit could decide upon a suitable present and constantly badgered me for suggestions.

In the end I was driven to protest.

'Look, Ran's taken Tamsin to see some friends of his and while they're gone I'm going to ice her cake. Why don't you two take the other car into Heraklion and have a look round the shops? I'm sure you'll be able to find something Tamsin would like—she isn't really very hard to please, you know!'

Melita's face lit up at the suggestion, but then she hesitated. 'Wouldn't you like to come with us, Annabel?'

I shook my head. 'No. I'd rather get the cake out of the way. Ran and Tamsin will probably be back before very long.'

I wasn't daft. I could see from Kit's and Melita's expressions that they were delighted at the prospect of being alone together and when a little later I saw them drive off I checked an involuntary sigh. I wasn't such a dog in the manger that I grudged Kit to Melita, but sometimes it was a little hard to remember that I didn't come first with him any more, and even harder to watch the happiness in Melita's face and the glow in her dark eyes.

When Venetia arrived, I thought wryly, I really would be out in the cold—though surely she and Ran wouldn't be stupid enough to let this most romantic of settings go to their heads and they'd continue to take care not to let Tamsin suspect how they felt about each other? It might not be easy, however: she was very young but also very perceptive.

I enjoyed icing the cake, especially as Sofia's kitchen, with the sun glinting on copper pots and bright chrome fittings, was a very pleasant room to work in. After I'd finished I would have liked to stay to chat to Sofia, who spoke English quite well, but it was obvious that she preferred to be left alone to start her preparations for the evening meal and so with an inward sigh I wandered into the garden.

I don't know why suddenly I was attacked by such an awful feeling of loneliness and despair. It had never ever happened to me before. But as I sat in that beautiful sunlit garden, so drenched in colour and sweet scents, I felt tears pricking my eyelids and suddenly I was crying, crying as I very rarely cried, weeping for my hopeless love, for Tamsin, for Kit and Melita, who had so many obstacles to face, and—oh, for so many nameless reasons!

I cried until I was utterly spent and exhausted and had just finished drying my eyes when to my horror I heard footsteps behind me and a moment later Ran's voice greeted me.

'All alone, Annabel? Where are Kit and Melita?'

Oh, dear God, if he saw my red and swollen eyes! I felt hot colour flooding my face and neck and carefully keeping my head averted I mumbled, 'They've —they've gone into Heraklion to choose a birthday present for Tamsin.'

'And you didn't go with them?' Ran's voice was sharp.

'Well, obviously I didn't.' I tried to laugh. 'I had Tamsin's cake to ice, you see.' And then, 'Where is she? I didn't expect you back quite so soon——'

'I left her with the Stephanos family. They have a little girl, Alexis, who's about Tamsin's age—they're going to play together.' I could feel Ran staring at me as he spoke and guessed that his brows were drawn together in his characteristic frown. I held my breath. Oh, if only he'd go away——

'Annabel, look at me.' It wasn't a request: it was an order. Then, as I said nothing but still kept my face averted, he bent down and taking hold of my wrists jerked me almost roughly to my feet. Then he tipped up my chin and I heard him catch his breath as he stared down at my tear-stained face. Anger blazed in his eyes.

'I thought so! You've been crying! My God, I'll break Kit's neck for this!' he said savagely. 'How dare he go off with Melita and leave you alone? How dare he hurt you?'

'Ran!' I felt my face grow even hotter as I realised why he thought I'd been crying. 'It—it isn't Kit's fault! I—I don't know why I cried! It was silly—there was absolutely no reason——'

'Rubbish! People don't cry for no reason—and especially not you, Annabel! I've seen you hurt . . . angry . . . in disgrace, but I've never seen you cry before!' Ran was still holding my wrists in a grip that hurt, but suddenly the ferocity died out of his face and his voice became gentle, his gaze as emotionally disturbing as a kiss.

'Annabel, don't be upset. I'll have a word with Kit. I won't let him treat you like this. The thing he's got about Melita, it can't be serious. She's much too young. It must be you he really wants——'

'Ran, don't!' The gentleness of his voice, the kindness of his eyes, unnerved me so much that to my horror I found myself in danger of weeping afresh. 'You don't understand! I don't want Kit and he doesn't want me and more than anything else in the world I don't want you to feel sorry for me!' I stopped. Then with a bitterness I could not hide I said, 'That's why you're being kind, isn't it—because you pity me! That's why you invited me to Greece in the first place! Well, you can keep your pity—I don't want it——'

There was a moment's silence. Then, very quietly, Ran said, 'Do you really think that the only reason I invited you to Greece was because I pitied you, Annabel? Do you really think that I'm being kind to you, as you put it, only because I feel sorry for you?' Then, as I did not immediately answer, 'Do you?'

I caught my breath in a sob. 'What other reason is there?' I asked wildly, trying to tug my hands free, and then, as I looked up into his face, my heart seemed to miss a beat. His eyes were blazing, with anger and with some other emotion that I didn't recognise.

'This!' he said harshly, and suddenly his arms went round me and his mouth came down on mine in a long hard kiss that seemed to last for ever. I could hardly bear the violence of that kiss or the emotion it aroused in me. I tingled and melted under his lips, feeling his heart beat madly against mine as if clamouring for admission.

'Well?' he asked hoarsely, holding me a little way away from him. 'Do you know now why I brought you to Greece? Do you still think that I feel sorry for you? Why, I've gone nearly out of my mind these last few days, thinking that you and Kit——' He stopped. 'Annabel, was that the truth you told me just now? Are you really not in love with Kit? Because if you aren't——'

I couldn't speak. I could only gaze at him dumbly, but perhaps my heart was in my eyes, for I heard him catch his breath.

'Annabel—darling Annabel——'

'*Kyrie*' That was Sofia's hesitant voice. '*Kyrie*, I am sorry, but there is someone here—she is asking to see you——'

I heard Ran swear softly under his breath as he released me and turned. Sofia was standing framed in an archway and there was someone behind her, someone dark and slender, who, as Sofia moved aside, came running to meet Ran with her hands outstretched.

'Ran! Oh, Ran!'

It was Venetia.

CHAPTER EIGHT

'VENETIA!' Ran's face was a study in blank astonishment. 'My dear, we didn't expect you until next week!' (My dear. Not my darling.) But then he knew that I was listening . . . and Sofia . . .

Venetia was half laughing, half crying. She flung her arms round Ran's neck and kissed his lean brown cheek. I wondered, with a strange feeling of unreality, whether she would notice the tiny smear of lipstick on his mouth.

'I know, but I had to come! I had to! Oh, Ran, I—I needed you so badly! There's something I——' She stopped. She must have read, as I did, the warning in Ran's eyes, for she seemed suddenly to become aware of my presence. She stared at me, her dark brows ever so slightly raised, and immediately I became acutely conscious of the fact that my dress was crumpled, my hair dishevelled, my eyes swollen and my face probably streaked with tears. A few moments ago I hadn't been worrying about any of those things, but now I felt utterly humiliated. I tried not to show it, though. I lifted my chin and said clearly, 'Hello, Venetia. I don't suppose you remember me, do you?'

'You must be Annabel.' Venetia was still staring at me. 'Ran told me that you were going to help him to look after Tamsin.'

'She's been invaluable.' Ran had recovered his *sang-froid*, and why not? I thought. Venetia was the third person who'd arrived unexpectedly : perhaps he was getting used to surprises by now. 'Tamsin adores her.'

His face was as impassive as his voice. Was it possible that I had imagined that passionate embrace only a few moments ago . . . the tenderness in his eyes . . . the way he'd held me, as though he never ever wanted to let me go ?

'I'm sure.' Venetia's tones were honey sweet, but they held a faint undertone of amusement. 'Annabel looks as though she hasn't changed a bit. I remember her as a real tomboy, all freckles and long legs and flying hair——'

She laughed, a soft, almost indulgent laugh that made me long to hit her. I drew a swift indignant breath, but Ran spoke before I did.

'Well, despite her present appearance, Venetia, I think you'll find she *has* changed, quite a bit,' he said, laughing, and I felt myself stiffen with disbelief. Oh, how *could* he laugh at me . . . how could he ? I wouldn't look at him. I knew that if I did he couldn't possibly fail to see the hurt in my eyes.

Coldly I said to Venetia, 'Tamsin will be simply delighted to see you. She did so want you to be here in time for her birthday, though Ran explained that it was quite impossible.'

'Her birthday !' Venetia's slender white hand flew to her mouth and she looked genuinely stricken. 'Oh, dear heaven ! I forgot ! It's tomorrow, isn't it ?' She turned to Ran, spreading out her hands in a gesture of appeal. 'What *am* I going to do ? I haven't bought the child a present !' Then, as if conscious of my scornful glance she added, reddening, 'I—I could only think about getting here as quickly as possible. It—

I haven't been very well, you see——'

I looked at her. At first I'd only been aware of the unpalatable fact that although it was quite a long time since I'd last seen her she was as beautiful as ever, her magnolia skin as perfect and luminous, her sleek black hair caught back in a heavy chignon, her figure slim and willowy. Now, though, I realised that she did look—not ill, but certainly fragile. There were violet shadows under her beautiful eyes as though she hadn't been sleeping well, and now that her lovely face was no longer irradiated by her joy at seeing Ran I saw that it bore unmistakable signs of tiredness and strain.

Ran looked concerned. 'I'm sorry to hear that, Venetia. Come into the house and sit down—you must be tired after your journey.' He took hold of her arm and spoke over his shoulder to Sofia, who was standing with her hands folded in front of her. 'Sofia, some of your special fruit juices for the *kyria*, please.'

'Oh, Ran! How good you are at looking after people!' Venetia gave him a grateful smile. 'This place is an absolute oasis—sheer heaven after New York, which was agony! I couldn't have borne it another day, I really couldn't.'

Ran's brows drew together in a slight frown. 'I gather you haven't finished your assignment?'

'No, but I'll tell you all about that later, Ran.' She put a gentle emphasis on the word 'you', subtly but effectively excluding me. 'What I'm craving for now is a cold drink—that orange juice sounds wonderful! —and then a shower and the chance to change my dress. I feel frightful!' she said, making an enchanting moue.

Of course she knew quite well she didn't look frightful at all, I thought bitterly, but when Ran said, 'Annabel, you'll show Venetia her room, won't you?' I answered readily.

'Of course.'

Sofia brought Venetia her orange juice in a long, frosted glass in which ice tinkled like little silver bells. Venetia sipped it with exclamations of delight and then I took her upstairs.

'I should think Tamsin will be home before very long,' I told her. 'And Kit and Melita, too.'

'Kit? Is he here?' Venetia raised her brows and then smiled. 'How nice for you, Annabel! And— Melita? Who is she?'

'Just a friend.' I had no intention of going into details—I'd leave that to Ran. 'If you're not down I'll send Tamsin up to you directly she comes in, shall I?'

Venetia hesitated. Then she said, plucking a little nervously at the skirt of her dress, 'Well . . . actually I rather thought that after I'd had a shower I might lie down and rest for a little while.'

'In that case I'll make sure she doesn't disturb you.' I had to exert all my will-power not to show my contempt. First she'd forgotten poor Tamsin's birthday and now, it seemed, she wasn't even anxious to see her.

Perhaps Venetia sensed my scorn, for she bit her lip and started to say something just as there was a knock at the door. It was Aristotle, with Venetia's three large cases and overnight bag, and I suddenly remembered what Tamsin had told me about her stepmother's excess baggage. I couldn't help wondering whether Ran realised that the beautifully cut silk suit that Venetia was wearing simply shrieked *haute couture* and that although she was wearing very little jewellery her ruby ring was undoubtedly real and so was her diamond bracelet. Whoever was married to Venetia had certainly got to be able to afford her . . .

Rather ashamed of the bitchiness of my thoughts I went into my own bedroom, closed the door and sat down on the bed. I knew that I ought to wash the tear-stains off my face, change my crumpled dress and then go downstairs and confront Ran, but suddenly I felt almost too tired to move. My cheeks were hot and I had the beginnings of a bad headache. Undoubtedly the dull pain in my temples was the result not only of my crying fit but of the tension I had felt ever since Venetia's inopportune arrival.

After a few moments I heard a knock at my door, followed by Ran's low voice.

'Annabel? Are you there?'

I sat absolutely still, not moving, not speaking, and after a little while Ran went away again. I found myself wondering, wearily, why he had bothered to kiss me. It seemed a long time ago . . . so long that I could scarcely remember what he had said to me. I could only remember Venetia's low, husky voice and her imploring, 'Ran, I had to come. I needed you so badly...'

Kit and Melita would be back at any moment. Stiffly, almost like an automaton, I rinsed my face, combed my hair, found a clean dress. It was an old cotton, a little faded, but that didn't matter, I told myself drearily. Whatever I wore, I couldn't possibly compete against Venetia. My mirror might show me the pleasing picture of a girl with zircon-bright eyes and a fall of honey-coloured hair, but if, like the wicked queen in the story of Snow White, I were to ask that same mirror, 'Mirror, mirror, on the wall, who is the fairest of them all?' I knew only too well what the answer would be. 'Venetia.'

And if I asked Ran the name of the woman he loved, would he say 'Venetia' too? Yes, of course he would, I thought, and sighed as I picked up my hair-brush. Romantic fool I might be, but there were limits to my romanticism—and to my foolishness.

I had just finished applying some make-up—a little more than usual, since my face still showed faint traces of tears—when Kit and Melita returned from Heraklion. They were flushed and gay and I could tell from a certain expression in Melita's sparkling eyes that they hadn't spent *all* their time wandering around the shops. I might have been a little worried if I hadn't been quite sure of Kit's intentions, but as it was I simply found myself hoping that Melita had enjoyed his kisses and that for her, at least, the sweet-ness would linger.

'Look! We have bought Tamsin a present between us,' she told me, and showed me a beautiful little glass horse that I knew Tamsin would love.

'It's enchanting.' I held the little model carefully, wondering as I looked at it what Venetia would do about Tamsin's present. Not, of course, that it really mattered very much. Venetia's presence on her birth-day would mean more to Tamsin than anything else.

'Venetia is here,' I told Melita, and was surprised how casual my voice sounded.

Melita looked surprised. 'Venetia? But I thought

she had to be in New York until next week!'

'Yes, but she decided to cut her stay short.' I hoped that Melita would not ask for explanations which in any case I was unable to supply.

Melita looked thoughtful. 'I am looking forward to seeing her. Kit says she is a—a knock-out!'

I laughed in spite of myself at her expression of triumph as she brought out the English slang word. 'Yes. Oh, yes, she's that all right,' I agreed.

I waited for Melita while she washed and changed and then we went downstairs together. Ran was in the *salotto*, pouring out drinks for himself and Kit. I felt his eyes on my face, but I deliberately didn't look at him. Instead I moved over to Kit's side and talked to him until a few minutes later Babis Stephanos brought Tamsin home.

Nobody told her that Venetia had arrived and was resting upstairs after her journey. She didn't know until in the midst of her excited account of her afternoon's activities she suddenly looked up and saw her stepmother standing in the doorway. She was wearing a low-cut black dress that showed off her magnolia skin, but even while paying a silent, grudging tribute to her beauty I found myself thinking that she still looked very tired.

'Tamsin darling!'

For a moment Tamsin stood rooted to the spot, her mouth wide open with amazement, then with a choked cry of, '*Venetia!* Oh, Venetia!' she hurled herself across the room and into her stepmother's waiting arms.

I waited cynically, for Venetia's anguished, 'Darling, be careful of my dress!' but instead she returned

Tamsin's hug with almost equal enthusiasm. Was she acting, I wondered, puzzled, or was she really fond of the child?

'Venetia, you'll be here for my birthday!' Tamsin kept saying over and over again, and Venetia laughed and kissed her.

'But of course, poppet! Such an important day ...'

So important that you'd forgotten all about it until I reminded you, I thought angrily, and looked away from Venetia and Tamsin to find Ran watching me intently. I couldn't read his expression, but I didn't return the little smile he gave me. After what had happened in the garden I didn't know where I stood any more. I was hopelessly confused. One moment I'd been happier than I'd ever been before in my life, knowing the enchantment, the wonderment, the magic of being in Ran's arms, then the next——

I sighed, and then quickly turned the sigh into a cough. No one must suspect for a single moment how miserable I felt—or that Ran was the reason. Ran and Venetia.

It was Melita who, during dinner, inadvertently caused Venetia a moment's embarrassment.

'Your husband ... he is a famous television producer, isn't he?' she asked. 'Will he be coming here to Crete to join you and Tamsin?'

Venetia had been smiling at something that Ran had said to her, but now the warmth died out of her face.

'No. No, I don't think so,' she said reluctantly. 'He's very busy ... he won't be able to get away.'

'But Daddy hasn't had a holiday this year.' Tamsin's voice was suddenly wistful. 'I wish you'd write to him and tell him how much we miss him, Venetia.'

'Darling, that wouldn't be any good.' Venetia's smile was a little forced. 'Daddy is making a film. He can't stop work until he's finished.'

'But you did!' Tamsin protested. 'You couldn't possibly have wanted to see me more than Daddy wants to see both of us!'

I saw Venetia go red and then white ... saw her dart an imploring look at Ran that was like a knife through my heart. *Rescue me*, it said.

Ran spoke quietly. 'Your father's work is very different from Venetia's, Tamsin. You know that.'

'Yes, but——'

Venetia interrupted her. Now quite in control of herself she said firmly, 'Tamsin, darling, have you finished your meal? Because if you have I really think you ought to go to bed. You've stayed up late tonight as a special treat, but I've no doubt that you'll be awake at the crack of dawn tomorrow and you ought to get at least a few hours' sleep!'

Tamsin didn't argue. 'Who's going to put me to bed —you or Annabel?' she asked, and I rose quickly to my feet.

'I'll see you into bed, Tamsin. That's my job.' I stressed the last word slightly and had the satisfaction of seeing Ran frown.

'All right. Well, I'll come up and kiss you good-night when you're ready,' said Venetia, smiling.

Tamsin gave a huge sigh of contentment when a few minutes later I tucked her up in bed.

'Oh, Annabel, hasn't this been a nice day? I'm so happy! I've made friends with Alexis, Venetia is here and tomorrow is my birthday! Oh, I feel as though I just can't wait!' She looked up at me, her eyes bright. 'I don't think I want you to read *The Hobbit* to me tonight, Annabel. I want to go to sleep as quickly as I possibly can!'

'That's a very good idea,' I agreed. I kissed her goodnight and then went downstairs to tell Venetia that she was ready.

Kit and Melita were in the *salotto*. It seemed as though they were arguing about something, for Melita's cheeks were flushed and her eyes dangerously bright and Kit looked distinctly unhappy. I couldn't help wondering what was wrong, but I didn't stop to ask any questions. I was too anxious to find Venetia.

'She's in the study with Ran, I think,' Kit said absently. And then, 'Do be reasonable, Melita——'

Suppressing an involuntary smile—for no one could be more unreasonable than Kit when he chose to be!—I crossed the hall and made my way towards the study, which was at the back of the villa. The door was half open and as I approached it I could hear the murmur of voices, Ran's low and deep, Venetia's soft and huskily alluring.

I didn't mean to eavesdrop, I swear I didn't. But as I raised my hand to tap on the door I distinctly heard Venetia say tearfully, 'Ran, it's no good. I *can't* tell Paul—I can't! He'll be so angry——'

'My sweet, you must.' Ran spoke firmly. 'Be sensible, Venetia. You can't possibly keep it a secret from him. However angry he is to begin with, he isn't an idiot, he knows quite well that these things do happen—it isn't your fault——'

'Yes, it is!' Venetia gave a despairing sob. 'Oh, Ran, I'm so frightened of telling him——'

I had been standing rooted to the spot, but now, as through the half-open door I saw Venetia go blindly into Ran's arms and bury her dark head on his shoulder I suddenly realised that I was very definitely an intruder. Neither of them had seen me. Choking back a gasp, I turned and fled into the garden, so filled with shame and anger and bitter disappointment that I wished I could run away for good.

Ran and Venetia were in love. There was no longer the slightest shadow of doubt in my mind. They were in love and Ran—Venetia's husband's best friend, Tamsin's godfather—was urging her to confess their secret to Paul. What other explanation could there be of his words—'These things do happen'? It was exactly what Kit had said aboard the *Ariadne*, when he'd been telling me that Paul's and Venetia's marriage was heading for the rocks and that Venetia wanted a divorce, so that she could marry Ran . . .

It was only now that I realised that in spite of everything I hadn't really believed him. I'd been sure, deep down in my heart, that Ran just wasn't capable of stealing another man's wife. Never mind that he'd known and loved Venetia first, long before she'd met Paul. It was Paul she had married, Paul to whom she had made her vows of love and fidelity and obedience. Not Ran. But . . . Paul was hundreds of miles away and Ran, at this moment, was holding Venetia in his arms, perhaps kissing her the way that earlier on he had kissed me. . . .

'*Why*? Why had he made love to me? I asked myself agonisedly. Was it just because he'd felt sorry for me? Had he meant to be kindly and comforting? Had that passionate kiss been in any way my fault . . . the way the first one, on Delos, had? I shivered. Maybe he guessed how much I loved him . . . guessed how much I wanted him . . .

I don't know how long I stayed in the garden. There was no moon tonight, just a dark blue sky pricked with stars. I looked for Scorpius. The sting of the scorpion . . . the heart of the scorpion . . . maybe, I thought bitterly, they were one and the same thing.

When I went inside again Kit was alone in the *salotto*.

'Where's Melita?' I asked.

'Gone to her room. I've upset her, I'm afraid.' Kit looked miserable.

I hesitated, then sat down beside him. 'Want to talk about it?'

Kit sighed. 'I suppose it might help. I didn't know until a few minutes ago, Annabel, but when Melita and I were in Heraklion this afternoon she bought a present for me as well as for Tamsin—a gold signet ring. Naturally she wanted me to wear it, and of course I had to tell her that it was out of the question. Ran knows damn well that at the moment I haven't got any money and if I suddenly start flaunting a new and very expensive-looking ring—well, it's obvious what he's going to think!'

He sighed again. 'Melita doesn't see that, though. The silly kid's got it into her head that I don't like her present and that she's gone and done something that she shouldn't have! Of course I've tried to convince her otherwise, but I haven't got very far. You women, you're so emotional——'

'I've told you before, Kit. Melita is very young.'

Kit looked gloomy. 'Well, what do I do? If I don't wear the blasted thing then Melita will break her heart and if I do Ran's almost bound to ask me where I got it from!'

'You could try telling him to mind his own business,' I suggested.

Kit gave me a rueful grin. 'He might think it *is* his business—since he felt so sorry for my impoverished state that yesterday he gave me three hundred drachmas! At times, you know, he can be surprisingly decent. Nevertheless, I think he'd be furious if he knew Melita had bought me such an expensive present, so whether she likes it or not I'm afraid she'll either have to keep it until such time as we can be officially engaged or else she'll have to take it back to the shop.' He paused as though a thought had suddenly struck him. 'Unless——'

I looked at him suspiciously. 'Unless what?'

'Unless I could somehow give him the impression that the ring was a present from *you*, Annabel? I needn't tell a direct lie——'

I was horrified. 'Oh no! Kit——'

'Annabel, please!' Kit spoke cajolingly. 'Ran won't care two hoots if he thinks you've given me the ring but Melita's a different matter. Like you said, he feels responsible for her. He's already suspicious——'

I gave an unsteady laugh. 'Not without reason! Kit, I don't like the idea of a deliberate deception——'

'But it's not going to harm anyone! Quite the opposite—Melita's going to be really unhappy unless I wear her ring. You and I know she's being unreasonable, but if it really means so much to her—Annabel, I just can't believe you won't help us! All we want to do is use you as a smokescreen——'

Smokescreen . . . I stared at him. I could hear foot-steps in the hall . . . Ran and Venetia? I thought of the way I had responded to Ran's kiss, how just for one magical moment I'd thought—I'd actually thought that——

My cheeks grew hot at the memory of my foolish-ness and recklessly I said, 'Well, the thicker the smokescreen the better. Maybe there won't be any need for Ran to ask questions when he sees that ring, Kit. Maybe, if he comes in now and finds you kissing me . . .' I put my hands on his shoulders and smiled up at him invitingly.

For a moment Kit looked completely nonplussed. Then a slow grin spread over his face and he put his arms around me. He was in the middle of kissing me —very thoroughly—when Ran and Venetia walked into the room.

'Oh—sorry!' said Venetia as we broke apart. And then, a little reproachfully, 'I thought you said you'd tell me when Tamsin was in bed, Annabel. She called me a few minutes ago and said she'd been waiting for me for ages!'

'Obviously,' said Ran in a very dry voice, 'Anna-bel has had other things on her mind.' His eyes met mine unsmilingly.

I had no need to pretend to be confused. 'Sorry, Venetia. Yes, I'm afraid it—it did slip my mind,' I confessed.

'No harm done.' Venetia looked from me to Kit and I could have sworn there was a hint of regret in her eyes. But why?

I said breathlessly, 'I must find Melita.' I couldn't

wait to get out of the room in order to escape Ran's searching gaze but he followed me.

'Annabel, I'd like a word with you, please.'

I halted my headlong rush and turned unwillingly. 'Ran, I'm in rather a hurry——'

'Rubbish. You certainly weren't in a hurry a few moments ago.' Ran's voice was grim and his stare almost accusing as he said, 'Don't you think you've got a bit of explaining to do?'

'Ex-explaining?'

'Don't try to look so innocent! I though you said —in the garden this afternoon—that you didn't want Kit and he didn't want you. So why the passionate clinch just now? You certainly looked as though you were enjoying yourselves.'

I caught my breath. It was too absurd. Ran couldn't be jealous—he just *couldn't* be! As nonchalantly as I could I said, 'This afternoon was this afternoon. Tonight was tonight——'

'Why were you crying?'

I swallowed. This was proving to be even harder than I'd expected it to be. 'Kit and I had a—a tiff. About Melita.' I was appalled to find how easily the glib lie tripped off my tongue. 'Then you came along——'

'The surrogate Prince Charming?'

'That's about it,' I agreed.

'I see,' Ran said slowly. He looked at me for a moment and then his mouth tightened. 'But you still haven't explained——'

'I don't think I owe you any explanation, Ran.' I was amazed how cool I sounded, though my mouth was dry and there was a sick feeling at the bottom of my stomach. 'Now, will you excuse me, please? I really must find Melita.'

I stepped past him. Halfway up the stairs I had a mad impulse to turn round, to say, 'Ran, it's not true. It's you I love, not Kit, but you're breaking my heart —you and Venetia——'

In fact, I *did* turn round. But Ran was already walking away and as I listened to the reverberations of his steps fading gradually away into the darkness I knew I lacked the courage to call him back, that whatever happened I would never be able to tell him how much I loved him.

CHAPTER NINE

TAMSIN'S birthday was as happy as I'd hoped it would be. Whatever storm clouds were gathering, her own small face was unshadowed as she received her greetings and presents and in typical Tamsin fashion thanked everyone by giving them a kiss and a rapturous hug.

Ran's gift was an enchanting musical box, Venetia's a tiny, heart-shaped locket which, she told Tamsin, had once belonged to her great-grandmother. I was surprised but glad that rather than be forced to admit to her stepdaughter that she had forgotten about her birthday Venetia had decided to part with one of her own treasured pieces of jewellery.

'Look, there's a space inside the locket for a photograph!' Tamsin gloated, her brown eyes sparkling. 'Whose shall I put in? Daddy's, I think.'

'Haven't you got a boy-friend yet?' Kit teased, and Tamsin tossed her head and shot him a quelling glance.

'No, I have not.'

'Pity. It's nearly always a boy-friend's photograph that a girl keeps in her locket,' Kit said solemnly, and Tamsin turned enquiringly to me.

'Is he joking, Annabel, or is that true? Have you got a photograph in your locket? Whose is it?' she demanded.

Blushing fierily, I put up my hand to my neck. I

was very fond of my little silver locket and though I
no longer wore it every day, as I'd done when I was
younger, I still wore it quite often. Some day, I supposed, I'd have to remove Ran's photograph, but there
didn't seem to be any particular hurry.

Now, conscious that everyone seemed to be waiting for my answer to Tamsin's question, I tried to prevaricate.

'Ah! That would be telling,' I said mysteriously.

'Is it Kit's?' Tamsin persisted, not easily put off.

'No. It's Mohammed Ali's,' I told her, and she
giggled.

'Oh, Annabel! I don't believe you!'

'Nor do I.' Kit, grinning and with an impish look in
his eyes, put out his hand and actually caught hold of
the locket before I realised what he intended to do.

'Leave it alone!' Apprehension made my voice
sharp. 'You'll break it!'

Kit withdrew his hand, staring at me in surprise.

'Okay, don't bite my head off——' he began, and
then, as if suddenly realising that Ran was watching
and listening, he added, 'There's no need to be coy,
darling,' and blew me a kiss.

Melita, who as yet knew nothing about the agreement that Kit and I had reached, coloured to the roots
of her hair and looked upset. I longed to kick Kit
under the table, but didn't dare. He really was an
idiot, I thought wrathfully.

Just then the telephone rang and a moment later
Sofia appeared to tell Tamsin that the call was for her.

'It is your father,' she announced, her face
wreathed in smiles, and Tamsin caught her breath.

'Daddy!' she exclaimed, her eyes shining like

stars, and her chair went flying as she jumped to her feet and raced for the door. Venetia, sitting next to me, gave a strangled gasp, and I noticed that her face had gone as white as a sheet as she looked imploringly at Ran.

'Ran, I can't talk to him! Not now! I can't.'

Ran shook his head. 'It's all right, Venetia. He doesn't know you're here, remember? I expect all he wants to do is to wish Tamsin a happy birthday,' he said gently.

There was an uncomfortable little silence as though we were all wondering why Venetia was so anxious not to speak to her husband. Kit's hand lay on the surface of the table, the gold signet ring winking in the sunlight. I saw Ran look at it, and then at me. I couldn't help it. I felt myself blushing fierily and he gave me a small nod as though he'd just had his unspoken question answered. I bent my head, longing for Tamsin's return. It could only have been a couple of minutes but it seemed like an age before she came dancing back into the room.

'I couldn't hear him very well 'cos the line was crackling, but I know he wished me a happy birthday,' she announced triumphantly. Her cheeks were flushed and she spoke in the breathless, non-stop way she had when she was very excited. 'I told him you were my best birthday present, Venetia, and I think he said why were you here, why weren't you still in New York, but when I asked if he wanted to speak to you the crackling suddenly got a lot worse and then the line just went dead.' She paused, then added sadly, 'I s'pose it's because Morocco's so far away.'

'I—I suppose so,' Venetia said faintly. Her face was

still very white and she seemed almost on the verge of tears.

Tamsin, sensitive as always to atmosphere, looked at her stepmother uncertainly.

'Venetia? Are you—is everything all right?'

'Quite all right.' Venetia gave her a brave smile. 'Have you finished your breakfast? Because if you have, Ran is going to take us into Heraklion. I noticed last night that you could do with a new pair of sandals—those are very badly scuffed, aren't they?'

'Oh, good! I like Heraklion.' Tamsin's face cleared and I drew a small sigh of relief as Kit said, 'Can I beg a lift, I meant to get a couple of films for my camera yesterday, but somehow I forgot.'

With Ran and Kit and Venetia all out of the way, I thought, there were certain things I could explain to Melita, whose face was still clouded. I'd wanted to talk to her the previous night, but after her quarrel with Kit she had locked her bedroom door and refused to answer to my knock.

'Look, Melita, you don't have to worry about me and Kit, I've told you that already,' I said bluntly when a few minutes later we found ourselves alone together. 'What's the matter? Aren't you sure of him?' Then, as she gave an almost imperceptible shake of her head, 'I don't see why not. He's wearing your ring, isn't he? If he seems to be—er—extra affectionate towards me when Ran is around it's because he wants him to think it's me he's interested in and not you.'

'Kit said last night we had to be very careful, but I don't see why,' Melita's relief was only partial. 'Why do we have to pretend?'

'Because you're very young, for one thing, and because Ran feels responsible for you for another. He doesn't want your parents to feel that he hasn't taken proper care of you, letting you fall in love with unsuitable young men——'

'Kit isn't unsuitable? He isn't! Annabel, how *can* you?' Melita protested spiritedly.

I sighed. 'Melita, he isn't rich—he hasn't even got a job at the moment——'

'I don't care whether he's rich or not and nor will my parents! As for a job—my father will find him one and Kit will do it well, because he now has something to work for! He never has before!'

'Yes, I believe you could be right,' I admitted. 'But Melita, are you sure that Kit is—well, the right person for you? You're only seventeen——'

Melita smiled. 'My sister Elena fell in love with her Andreas when she was only sixteen. I am not too young to be sure that my feelings for Kit will never change, Annabel.'

I opened my lips to argue but then closed them again. How old had I been when I'd first fallen in love with Ran? And had I changed *my* mind? Of course I hadn't. So why should I worry that Melita might?

'Well, you do see the necessity for discretion, I hope?' I tried hard to sound severe. 'There's no need to rush things, you know. You'll only make things difficult for everyone. You wouldn't like Ran to send Kit away——'

Melita looked alarmed. 'Do you really think he might?'

'Yes, I do, if he thought that things were in danger of—er—getting out of hand. There'd better not be any more expensive presents, for instance——'

Melita went scarlet. 'No. There won't be.' She hesitated. 'I thought—I thought Kit said last night he couldn't wear my ring, in case Ran asked awkward questions——'

'You needn't worry. I'm pretty sure that Ran thinks I gave the ring to Kit. I just hope he doesn't ask me outright, that's all. I don't like lies——'

I stopped, suddenly ashamed of myself. What a hypocrite I was! I'd already lied to Ran about Kit. I'd been so desperate last night to hide my disappointment, my hurt, that I hadn't cared what I'd said. No wonder pride was counted as one of the seven deadly sins . . .

Melita was looking at me with unusual thoughtfulness. 'You're too old for Kit, Annabel,' she said suddenly. 'Me, I am just the right age.'

I pretended to be affronted, 'What do you mean—too old? I'm several months younger than Kit!'

Melita shook her head. 'You are still too old for him. It is Ran who would be exactly right for you, Annabel. I do wish——' It was her turn to stop.

'You wish what?' I asked in a tight-sounding voice.

'Nothing. I've forgotten what I was going to say. Come on, let's go down to the beach. It's too hot to do anything else.'

I assented, and we were still soaking up the sun when the others returned from Heraklion. Kit, Venetia and Tamsin joined us on the beach, but Ran claimed that he had some letters to write and Venetia did not stay long with us, either. She refused to swim, saying that she did not feel energetic enough and indeed she still didn't look well. Her pallor was even more pronounced than it had been the previous day and she seemed content to lie on the beach with her eyes closed. The sun glinted on her dark hair, her slender, graceful limbs and the plain gold ring she wore on the third finger of her left hand. Paul's ring.

'Venetia, I want to show you something!' After a few minutes Tamsin grabbed hold of her arm and Venetia sighed and opened her eyes.

'Oh, Tamsin, must I move?'

'Yes, you must,' Tamsin said ruthlessly, and dragged her stepmother off to show her a tiny rock pool in which she had imprisoned a couple of baby crabs. I frowned to myself as I watched them go. There was something about Venetia that for some peculiar reason aroused my sympathy. I wanted to hate her but instead, much against my will, I found myself feeling sorry for her. She was so obviously worried and unhappy that somehow I knew that whatever she had decided to do about her marriage she had not made the decision lightly.

It was because of those reluctant stirrings of sympathy that when she came back, dragging her footsteps a little, I said impulsively, 'Don't let Tamsin wear you out. Say "no" to her sometimes. She's got so much energy that it's impossible for anyone to keep up with her.'

For a moment Venetia looked surprised and then she smiled. 'Yes, she *is* energetic, isn't she? She's just like——' She stopped.

'Her father?'

'Yes!' Was it my imagination, or was there more than a hint of wistfulness in Venetia's voice? 'He's always been terribly restless ... so different from Ran. Yet they're such good friends——'

I said nothing. Paul's and Ran's friendship had survived even after Paul had married the girl Ran loved, but would it—could it—still survive if Ran took her back again?

I looked a little desperately to where Kit and Melita and Tamsin were playing beachball. I didn't want to talk about Ran, so I brought the subject back to Tamsin.

'She's a darling, really. I've grown very fond of her,' I said, and Venetia stretched out her slender hands and studied her red-painted nails.

'She's very fond of you, too. You and Ran have been wonderfully kind to her. I'm so glad he thought of asking you along.'

'Me, too.' I spoke lightly.

There was an odd silence. Then carefully, almost as if groping for words, Venetia said, 'Ran isn't an easy person to get to know, but he's one of the nicest, kindest men I've ever met.' She hesitated, then smiled faintly. 'Still, I don't suppose I have to tell you that, do I? You know him as well as I do.'

'I doubt it.' I spoke coldly. I hated having to discuss Ran at all, but especially with Venetia.

Venetia arched her brows. 'But good heavens, you've been in and out of the Hall all your life! You always seemed to be around whenever I used to visit——'

'It was Kit I went to see, not Ran.' As I spoke I caught Kit's eye and he smiled and waved and I smiled back. It took me completely by surprise when Venetia said with sudden vehemence, 'Ran's worth two of Kit! Oh, Annabel, can't you *see* that?'

For a moment I was speechless, then anger flooded me. How dared she? Oh, how *dared* she?

I took off my sunglasses and glared at her. 'And is he worth two of Paul, too?' I asked softly, and gave her full marks for her blank, astonished stare. She wasn't only a good model, she was a good actress as well, I thought bleakly, and getting up I stalked towards the water's edge. Tamsin came running to join me, squealing with delight when I threatened to duck her, and when I looked round, a few minutes later, Venetia had gone.

Because it was Tamsin's birthday, Ran had promised her that we would all go out for a meal in a local *taverna* where there was *bouzouki* music and dancing. Of course she was thrilled at the prospect of such a grown-up treat, but she also seemed to enjoy the tea-party which Sofia and I had planned for her long before Venetia's arrival. It was a noisy, happy celebration and the food disappeared with such astonishing rapidity that Ran laughingly suggested that no one would have room for any dinner.

'Don't you believe it!' said Kit, grinning. 'That was a mere snack!—Annabel, my love, congratulations! The birthday cake was a dream!'

'It certainly was.' Venetia gave me her lovely smile. 'You're full of surprises, Annabel. I never knew you were domesticated.'

I inclined my head politely and picked up a tray of china, meaning to carry it back to the kitchen. Ran followed me outside.

'I've been meaning to have a word with you, Annabel, about the salary I promised you,' he said in a cool, impersonal-sounding voice. 'I've paid you nothing as yet but I think it's high time I did, don't you?' He held out a small white envelope. 'I hope you'll find the remuneration adequate.'

I felt the colour flood into my face. 'Ran, I told you I didn't want a salary! You've—you've already been more than generous——'

Ran interrupted me. 'The money you brought with you must be running out. I heard you telling Tamsin today that you couldn't afford to have your hair done in Heraklion, and I don't want your holiday to be spoilt by penny-pinching.' He paused. 'Though of course, if you *will* buy such expensive presents——'

He was referring to the ring, of course. The ring he thought I'd given Kit. There was nothing I could say. Miserably clutching the envelope he had pushed into my hands, I watched him turn on his heel and walk back into the *salotto*.

'Oh, Annabel, do you suppose he thinks you and Kit are as good as engaged?' Melita asked, wide-eyed, when a little later I told her about the incident. Then, as I shrugged without answering, 'You don't like deceiving him, do you, Annabel? I'm sorry. It's all right for Kit and me, but I've been thinking. What do you suppose will happen when Ran finds out about Kit and me eventually? Won't he—won't he be terribly angry with you for what you've done?'

'Probably.' I spoke lightly, not wanting to let Melita know that that was something I tried hard not to think about. With any luck, though, by the time Ran realised that Kit and I had pulled the wool over his eyes I'd be back at university and I probably wouldn't see him again for ages. Especially if he went to Las Palmas—and Venetia joined him. It didn't take long to obtain a divorce these days, not if both parties agreed . . .

It was Venetia who later dressed Tamsin for her 'grown-up' party and I had to admit she made a really good job of it. She wore a turquoise embroidered caftan and her hair, released from its usual pony-tail, fell like a scarf of shining silk on to her slender shoulders.

'How pretty you look!' I told her, and she flushed with pleasure.

'You look pretty, too, Annabel.'

I smiled a little wryly. I had certainly taken trouble with my appearance, but it seemed to me that beside Venetia and Melita, with their dramatic colouring, my honey-coloured hair and blue eyes must look insipid . . . nondescript.

Ran had asked Loukas Stephanos, Alexis' elder brother, to join us at the *taverna*, evidently with the intention of pairing him with Melita. He was an attractive young man, with a pleasant smile and an engaging manner, but although I could see that he hoped to captivate Melita I knew that he was simply wasting his time. She had made up her mind that she wanted Kit, and Kit she intended to have.

Tamsin was enchanted with everything—the *taverna* itself, with its candlelit tables, the small orchestra playing *bouzouki* music, and the other diners, who divided their time between eating and dancing with the wild vitality which made me remember that Ran had once remarked that the Greeks were born to dance—they started in their cradles.

Venetia, beautiful in a flame-coloured dress, her dark hair piled like a crown of jet on top of her shapely head, danced several times with Ran and I tried hard not to watch them. They made such a handsome pair, and they moved perfectly in time with the loud rhythm of the music.

It was Tamsin who pointed out, halfway through the evening, that Ran had not yet asked me to dance. It was an awkward moment, but Ran rose unhesitatingly to the occasion.

'I thought Annabel would probably be happier dancing with Kit, Tamsin. However, if she would like a change of partner for once——?' He looked enquiringly at me.

There was no help for it. I rose reluctantly to my feet and Ran's lips quirked as he led me out on to the floor.

'Such enthusiasm,' he murmured.

I didn't answer. Tight-lipped, I felt him draw me into his strong, muscular arms, though to my relief he didn't try to hold me closely. We circled the floor once or twice, then rather abruptly Ran said, 'Annabel, there's something I want you to know.'

My heart missed a beat. Was he going to tell me about himself and Venetia? I moistened my lips nervously. 'Yes?'

Ran drew a long breath. 'There's no reason why the Hall should remain empty if I decided to go to Las Palmas. You and Kit could live there if you wanted to. You'd be near your parents, which I'm sure they'd like very much, and I suppose Kit could find himself some job or other.'

I could taste the acid in my mouth. This was taking

deception too far. Ran was being nice ... kind ... kinder by far than I deserved. He didn't know I was a liar and a cheat. Not yet.

'Ran, I don't know ... Kit and I have made no plans at all,' I stammered. And then, 'We couldn't possibly take your home from you———'

'I'd like to think of your living there. And it would make you happy, wouldn't it? You've always loved the old place,' Ran said quietly, and I had to bend my head so that he wouldn't see the tears that pricked my eyes.

Just then the music stopped. For a moment Ran stood lightly holding my wrists with his hands, then he turned and led me back to our table, where Kit was waiting to claim the next dance.

Shortly after that he and Venetia left to take Tamsin home to bed. They didn't return, and when Kit and Melita and I arrived at the villa, around about midnight, the whole house was in darkness.

CHAPTER TEN

THE advent of Venetia brought, as I'd expected, several changes. She, Ran and Tamsin spent most of their time swimming and sunbathing, and only rarely joined in the sightseeing trips that the rest of us—for a variety of reasons—always enjoyed.

Basically, of course, Kit and I found it a relief not to have to worry about putting on an act for Ran's benefit. We all felt the strain of that, but me especially, because unlike Kit and Melita I felt terribly guilty about the deception we were practising. I wished, now, that I had never let myself become so deeply involved, although I couldn't help realising that I had only myself to blame. What was it Sir Walter Scott had said?

> 'O what a tangled web we weave
> When first we practise to deceive . . .'

Well, this was a tangled web all right, so tangled that for the first time I began to think that I would be glad when the holiday was over. Everything had been so wonderful to begin with, but now—well, now it was all spoilt.

My only consolation was that Tamsin seemed much happier. Even though she still missed her father, she had her adored Venetia, and I was surprised to see how genuinely fond of her small stepdaughter Venetia seemed to be. In fact, Venetia herself surprised me because she was quite unlike my imaginary picture of her, gentler and kinder than I would have believed possible. She still looked tense and worried, though, and I was pretty sure that Ran was worried, too. In spite of everything my heart ached for him. He was in a dreadful position, torn as he was between his love for Venetia and his loyalty towards his friend, and I couldn't help wishing that there was something I could do to make things easier for him.

There wasn't of course. He had very little to say to me and seemed, I thought, to be avoiding me whenever he could. His indifference hurt me and I had to work really hard at being gay and cheerful so that no one should suspect that I wasn't, after all, having the holiday of a lifetime.

I had sent a long letter home, describing the things I had seen and done, and in return I received one from Mother telling me about the dreary visit she and my father had paid to my Aunt Isobel and bemoaning the fact that ever since they had returned home it had rained, non-stop, practically every single day.

I read the letter as I lay sprawled on baking hot sand beneath a row of jagged black cliffs, with the blue, blue sea sparkling invitingly only a little way away. For the first time since we had come to Crete we had deserted our own little private beach in favour of another further along the coast. It was close to a little fishing village and after we had had our fill of sunbathing we meant to stroll along to the harbour and watch the brown-skinned fishermen unloading their colourful caiques.

It was so hot that only Tamsin had any inclination to explore. Venetia and Ran were lying side by side with their eyes shut, Melita was rubbing herself with oil and Kit was tracing patterns on the sand with a small stick. I hoped he would remember not to do anything silly, like writing 'K.A. loves M.M.'

I finished reading Mother's letter and was about to stuff it into my beach bag when I saw Tamsin racing towards us, her face blazing with excitement.

'Ran! Venetia! Oh, everyone, do come quickly! I've found a super little path, it leads right the way up the cliff and there's a little ruined temple at the very top!' she panted. 'Oh, it's simply lovely! Please come and look!'

Everyone groaned in unison, but it was impossible to resist the appeal in her big brown eyes. None of us really felt like toiling up a steep path just to see another pile of ruins, but we all scrambled to our feet, even Venetia. Ran, however, did sound a note of caution.

'I wonder if your little path is safe, Tamsin? It looks as though this place is subject to quite severe rock falls from time to time,' he said, frowning at the big boulders which were strewn at the bottom of the jagged cliffs.

'Well, Tamsin seems to have been up and down the path without bringing half the cliff down on our defenceless heads!' Kit said, laughing. 'Now that I'm up I'd like to see your temple, Tamsin, so lead the way!'

'I'd like to see the temple, too,' Melita agreed, and Ran shrugged and said no more. He knew quite well that Kit always opposed him if he could and that argument was probably useless.

The path that Tamsin had found was nearly as

steep as the one we had climbed at Santorin and the going wasn't at all easy, but the view, when we finally reached the top, was breathtaking. There was a hot, heady scent of pine and thyme and amidst the ruins of the tiny temple wild flowers grew—rock roses, anemones and hyacinths, while here and there a huge, ghostly-looking asphodel thrust up from the bare, rocky earth.

'Look! There's the fishing village! Doesn't it look tiny, Melita?' Tamsin, searching for familiar landmarks, was all eagerness.

I turned, and with memories of Sounion crowding into my mind meant to caution her not to go near the edge, but just at that moment Kit called me to where he and Ran were inspecting a broken column.

'Look at this, Annabel. It's a carving of some kind or another, but neither of us can quite make it out. Is it meant to represent someone on horseback, do you think?'

I bent to look at the weatherbeaten stone and as I did so the air was split by a terrified scream. I spun round, my heart standing still, and to my horror saw Tamsin disappearing over the edge of the cliff as the ground on which she was standing suddenly gave way. Melita, standing just behind her, made a frantic grab at her dress, missed her footing and the next moment she, too, slithered over the edge. There was a shrill, choked-off scream, the crash of stone on stone, and then a horrible, deathly silence.

It all happened with such terrifying speed that for a moment I think we were all completely paralysed. Ran was the first to move. His face grey under his tan, he flung himself flat on the edge of the cliff and peered over. Instinctively I shut my eyes, expecting every moment that there would be another rock slide, but there was nothing save a cascade of small pebbles.

Venetia, her face horror-stricken, gave a little moan. 'They're dead! They must be! Oh, how can I ever tell Paul?' she sobbed, and clutched hold of my arm as if for support.

'They can't be dead!' Kit, who had been standing like a man turned to stone, suddenly strode forward and flung himself down beside his brother. The next moment we heard Ran call out, and however he felt his voice sounded strong and reassuring.

'Hold on, Melita! Don't move! You're going to be all right!' Then hoarsely, for our benefit, he said, 'They're lucky—they haven't fallen very far. Tamsin's on a fairly broad ledge and as long as she doesn't move she'll be all right. She's alive—I saw her foot move—but I think she may be only semi-conscious——'

'And—and Melita?' I felt deathly cold, but strangely calm, unlike Venetia, who had crumpled into a little heap and was sobbing brokenly.

'She's clinging to a rock just above the ledge. No, keep back, Annabel!' as I moved forward. 'Stay where you are!—Kit, that rock isn't safe. I saw it shift: I don't think it's going to hold much longer. I'm going down, try to guide Melita on to the shelf——'

'No!' Kit spoke savagely. 'No, Ran! That's my job! I'm going down——'

'You young fool! This is no time for heroics!' Ran blazed, but Kit cut him short.

'I've got the right to go! Not you!' he said in a

voice I'd never heard him use before. 'Ran, you don't understand! That's my girl down there—the girl I'm going to marry! Do you think I'm going to let anyone else risk his neck for my girl?'

Just for a moment the silence was electric as the two brothers stared at each other. Then, with a brief nod of understanding, Ran turned to me.

'Okay, Kit, get moving. Annabel, you'll have to get help as quickly as you can—men with ropes. But for God's sake, my dear, be careful——'

For an instant our gaze met and it was as though a silent question flashed between us. I didn't try to interpret it; there wasn't time. I was already making for the cliff path. I tried not to think about Kit and the danger he was facing but to concentrate instead on my own vertiginous descent. The path had been treacherous enough coming up, but now, because I was running, it was doubly so. Loose scree slipped and slithered beneath my sandalled feet and twice I tripped and sprawled forward violently. Each time the breath seemed to have been knocked out of my body and the throbbing pain in my hands and knees made me vaguely realise that they were torn and bleeding, but somehow I went on running. Slower, though, now, much slower, because I had an agonising stitch in my side and there seemed to be bright lights dancing in front of my eyes and a strange buzzing in my ears. How much further? Oh, how much further?

I couldn't really believe it when at last I felt soft sand beneath my feet instead of the stony path. I stood for a moment sobbing for breath, my left knee a fury of protest. The fishing village ... men with ropes . . . I'd only accomplished half my mission. But the going would be a little easier now. Help was only minutes away. If only—if only I knew it wasn't already too late.

'Annabel—oh, Annabel! You were wonderful! Help came long before we felt we could possibly expect it —you must have run like the wind before you hurt your knee! Ran says how you didn't break your neck going down that awful path he'll never know!'

A long time later, when it was all over and Kit and Melita and Tamsin were safe and sound, Venetia sat beside me in my pretty blue-and-white bedroom at the Villa Samphira and looked at me with big dark eyes that were unusually bright. She might have gone to pieces at the time of the accident, but she had made up for it ever since. I had protested vehemently about being sent to bed, but the doctor who had bandaged my bleeding knees and hands had impressed upon Venetia that I needed rest and she had bullied me so much that in the end I had given in.

Now I smiled a little ruefully. 'It wasn't the path that was so awful, Venetia. It was not knowing—not knowing if——'

Venetia put out her hand and clasped mine firmly. 'Don't think about it any more, Annabel. Melita is safe, thanks to Kit, and so is Tamsin, though she's still badly shocked, poor darling. However, when I think how lucky she is still to be alive——' She shuddered.

I moved restlessly. 'Tell me again what happened after I'd gone for help, Venetia. Kit climbed down to help Melita on to the ledge . . . is that right?'

'Yes, and it's a good thing he did, for the rock she

was clinging to became dislodged seconds after they
were both safely on the ledge,' Venetia said soberly.
'Luckily, Tamsin was unconscious. She knew nothing
at all until she woke up in hospital to find herself with
two cracked ribs and a very sore head. I'm afraid,
though, it will be a long time before she forgets the
sheer horror of finding herself falling into space——'

'Isn't there anything anyone can do to take her
mind off it?' I asked anxiously, and Venetia hesitated.
Then quietly she said, 'Paul . . . my husband . . . should
be here very soon. I wanted to see him about—about
something very important and Ran thought I should
phone him and ask him to come. I made the call yesterday, long before the accident happened.' She
paused, then added, 'I'm glad I did. Tamsin adores her
father: seeing him will give her more happiness than
anything else in the world.'

I tried not to think about the implications of
Venetia's phone call to her husband. 'Yes, I think
you're right. But isn't your husband still filming?'

'He said he could get away for a day or two. Apparently shooting's been held up, anyway, something
to do with a strike.'

I raised my brows. 'In Morocco?'

Venetia gave a faint smile. 'You can have a strike
anywhere these days, Annabel—except perhaps behind the Iron Curtain.' She rose to her feet and stood
looking down at me. 'You're supposed to have peace
and quiet and that really means no visitors, but Kit
and Melita want to see you so badly that I had to
agree. I think they want to make quite sure you really
are all right.'

'Good heavens! It was Melita who went over the

cliff, not me! She's the one who ought to be in bed,'
I said, laughing, but when Venetia had gone I buried
my face in my pillow. What about Ran? Didn't he
want to see me? Did he find it impossible to forgive
me for deceiving him?

Melita and Kit crept into my bedroom hand-in-
hand and stood looking down at me. Melita, astonish-
ingly very little the worse for her experience, said,
'Annabel, isn't it marvellous? Kit saved my life! He's
a hero!'

'Rubbish!' Kit protested, flushing to the roots of his
fair hair and looking acutely uncomfortable. 'You do
exaggerate, Melita!' He hesitated, then said awkwardly, 'I'm afraid I gave the show away, Annabel.
To Ran, I mean. I was so scared about Melita——'

'I know. I heard you.' I gave a shaky laugh. 'How
has Ran reacted since?'

Kit's face lit up. 'Incredibly well! Oh, he asked
how long you'd known that I was in love with Melita
and he seemed a bit shaken when I told him I'd put
you in the picture from the very beginning, but otherwise he couldn't have been nicer.' He added sheep-
ishly, 'I—I think perhaps Ran and I will be better
friends in future, Annabel. Somehow what's happened seems to have brought us closer together. He
—he isn't such a bad sort after all. He's even been in
touch with Melita's parents——'

'With the result that they are so grateful to Kit for
saving my life that I don't think they will object at
all to the prospect of his becoming their son-in-law!'
said Melita, her dark eyes dancing. 'Kit is coming back
with me to Mykonos, and although he says he is not

a hero I think he will be given a hero's welcome!'

I smiled. I was glad for their happiness: I really was. But somehow, even though Ran had forgiven Kit, I didn't think it likely that he had forgiven me . . .

He came to see me that afternoon. I heard him coming from a long way off: even the sound of his footsteps was unique, I thought, trembling. My heart was beating fast, but not with pleasurable anticipation.

Ran stood at the foot of my bed, his dark face unsmiling.

'Venetia tells me you're feeling much better.'

'Yes,' I said quietly.

A little muscle twitched in Ran's cheek. 'I don't suppose I need tell you how grateful I am to you for fetching help so quickly. All the same, I did tell you to be careful.' He sounded angry. 'You might have killed yourself——'

'Well, I didn't, did I?' I took refuge in defiance. 'I'm perfectly all right. I don't know why that silly doctor insisted on my staying in bed——'

Ran smiled unwillingly. 'I think he knew what he was doing. Annabel——'

I held my breath. 'Yes?'

'Why did you lie to me? Was it because you thought I'd disapprove if I knew the truth about Kit and Melita?'

My throat felt tight. 'Yes,' I muttered.

'Well, you were right . . . up to a point. But I'm not an ogre, Annabel, and believe it or not Kit's happiness is quite important to me.' Ran looked at me with a coldness that hurt worse than my knee. 'Did it never occur to you that I might disapprove of lies and deceit rather more than I disapproved of two young people falling in love?'

I didn't say anything. I couldn't. There was a long silence. Then Ran, turning towards the door, said in a voice that sounded oddly tired, 'Your loyalty to Kit is to be commended, I suppose, Annabel. You may not be in love with him, but it's pretty obvious that he's still the most important person in your life next to your parents. I thought for a little while—but I was wrong about that, apparently. My fault, not yours.'

Wrong about *what*? I had been staring down at my clasped hands, but now I raised my head, a bewildered question trembling on my lips. I never voiced it, for Ran was already closing the bedroom door behind him and a moment later I heard him speaking to Sofia. She had brought me a pot of English tea and some of her special biscuits: she meant to be kind, but I didn't want the biscuits and by the time I drank the tea it was salted with my tears.

Paul arrived at the villa two days later and we were all relieved to see him. The nurses at the hospital had told Venetia that Tamsin had had dreadful nightmares two nights running and they were hoping that her father's presence would calm and soothe her.

The first evening I didn't see much of Paul, for he and Venetia spent nearly a couple of hours at their ecstatic daughter's bedside. I realised that it was unlikely that Venetia would talk to her husband about their marriage while Tamsin remained a source of anxiety, but I guessed that she was feeling very much on edge, for she was exaggeratedly bright and brittle. Between her and Paul there seemed to be a barrier very similar to that which existed between Ran and myself and I almost found myself wishing that she would hurry up and tell him that she wanted her freedom. At least it would clear the air, if nothing else.

Not that Ran seemed particularly uptight. He acted towards Paul as though he had absolutely nothing to feel ashamed of and every time I saw the two men laughing and talking together my bewilderment increased. How could you plan to steal your best friend's wife and not feel a heel for doing it? Did Ran think along the lines that he was merely getting his own back?

I tried, in a roundabout way, to find out what Kit thought about the situation, but he and Melita were so wrapped up in each other that I just couldn't get him on his own for a private conversation. They were full of plans for the future and I was amused to see how already Kit seemed older and more responsible. The chances were that marriage to Melita would be the making of him: I thought it likely that in the end they would be extremely happy.

'Kit says he will take me to England for our honeymoon,' Melita announced, her eyes sparkling. 'I shall like that very much. I want to see Kit's old home—and yours too, Annabel.'

We were all having lunch at the time and I was about to make some lighthearted rejoinder when I suddenly noticed that Venetia, who had been very silent throughout the meal, had risen somewhat unsteadily to her feet. Her face was paper-white and she swayed so much that she had to cling to the table for support.

'I'm sorry—I don't feel well,' she said in a small

voice, and just for a moment she looked as though she was going to faint.

'Venetia!' Paul, sitting next to her, sprang to her assistance and for the first time since his arrival at the villa I saw an emotion other than concern for his little daughter flicker across his lean features. There was real anxiety in his eyes as he put his arm round Venetia's slim shoulders and when he spoke his voice was warm and reassuring.

'It's all right, darling. Hold on to me. You've nothing to worry about—I won't let you fall.'

Venetia leant heavily against her husband, her face still completely colourless.

'I—I feel so dizzy. I think I'd better go and lie down,' she murmured weakly, and evidently Paul agreed with her, for without a moment's hesitation he scooped her up into his arms and carried her out of the room.

There was an awkward little silence after they'd left. I glanced covertly at Ran beneath my lashes and saw that he was gazing down at his wine glass with an odd expression on his face. He said nothing, however, and it was Melita who spoke first.

'Poor Venetia! She has been so worried about Tamsin! I expect she is feeling the effect of all the tension,' she murmured, and I bit my lip. Venetia had been tense and worried long before Tamsin's accident!

'I wonder—do you think perhaps Paul needs any help?' I asked hesitantly, and Ran shook his head.

'He'll ring for Sofia if he does. I shouldn't worry, Annabel.' He hesitated, then glanced at his watch. 'The only thing is, they've promised to be at the hospital by three o'clock and Tamsin will be frantic if one of them at least doesn't turn up. Venetia may not feel up to a visit, so if it's necessary could you stay with her while Paul goes, Annabel?'

'Of course.'

There was no need for Ran to point out to me how disappointed Tamsin would be if her beloved father was even a few seconds late, and so when by quarter to three there was no sign of either Paul or Venetia emerging from their room I decided, somewhat reluctantly, that I would have to knock on the door.

Paul's deep voice bade me enter, but it was a few seconds before I could summon up the courage to do so. Subconsciously, I think perhaps I was afraid of seeing a weeping Venetia and an angry Paul, but instead I received the shock of my life.

Venetia was sitting curled up in her husband's lap, one slender arm curved round his neck and her lovely face alight with so much happiness that I could only stand and stare. Where were the lines of stress and worry? Her eyes were rapt and shining and there was a tender curve to her lips. She looked a different woman.

For a moment sheer surprise held me speechless, then belatedly I remembered my errand. Scarlet-cheeked, I stammered, 'Paul, Ran asked me to remind you that Tamsin will be expecting you at three and that she'll be terribly upset if you're late.'

'Too true.' Venetia looked up at her husband with a gay softness in her eyes and he responded with a quick smile.

'I'd like you to stay here, darling, and rest a little longer. I'll tell Tamsin our good news—unless you want to tell her yourself, that is?'

Venetia shook her head as gracefully she uncurled herself. 'No, you tell her, Paul. Tell her all our plans and then I think she'll have happy dreams instead of nightmares.'

She looked smilingly at me as Paul kissed her again and then, whistling cheerfully, took his departure.

'Annabel! Oh, Annabel, you look so surprised!'

With an effort I pulled myself together. 'I—I thought you were feeling ill——'

'Not ill,' said Venetia laughing. 'Just a little faint, that's all—and for the very best possible reason!' I stared at her. 'You mean——?'

'I mean I'm going to have a baby!' Venetia gave a soft, exultant laugh. 'Oh, Annabel, I can't tell you how happy I am! I've been so frightened of telling Paul—I was sure he'd be so angry with me——'

'Angry?' My voice, even to my own ears, sounded utterly bewildered.

Venetia sat down on the bed. 'Maybe I ought to explain,' she said soberly. 'Annabel, you know what happened to Tamsin's mother, don't you? She died giving birth to Tamsin. It shattered Paul at the time —it was stupid, but he blamed himself for Louise's death. When he fell in love with me, he never expected that I'd want a child—but I did, Annabel, I wanted a baby terribly! I'd—I'd always dreamed of having a family and I was heartbroken when I discovered that Paul was dead against having any more children at all. He—he was afraid of losing me, you see, the way he lost Louise——'

She stopped. Then she said ruefully, 'We argued about it continually. I did everything I could to try and make him change his mind, but he was adamant. Our marriage really was under a pretty severe strain —in fact, if it hadn't been for Ran, who was a wonderful friend to us both, I think we might have parted. We both owe him so much—what's the matter, Annabel? Why are you looking like that?'

I shook my head. 'It doesn't matter. Go on, Venetia.'

'There isn't very much more. Paul went off to Morocco and in sheer desperation I took up modelling again, though I never really cared for it. I was offered the New York assignment and it was while I was there that I discovered that I was pregnant.' A rueful smile curved Venetia's lips. 'At first I was overjoyed, but then I realised that Paul would probably think I'd planned it and be so furiously angry with me for disregarding his wishes that there'd be no future for us at all. I came here to Ran, to ask him what I should do. He—he knew what I was contemplating, I think, and he told me not to be an utter fool, that Paul loved me and that once he knew the baby was on the way he'd probably be over the moon.' She laughed. 'And he was right. I told Paul the truth a little while ago and he said—oh, Annabel, I won't tell you what he said, but I'm so happy I could *burst*!'

I looked at her and kept on looking. I was so suffused with shame that although I opened my mouth twice I couldn't frame the words. Then I took a deep breath and said, 'Tamsin will be happy, too. She—she's been so worried about you and Paul——'

'She'll love to have a baby brother or sister. Paul is going to take us both back to Morocco with him and then, when his work there is finished, we're going to look for a house in the country. Paul says babies don't belong in flats, and of course they don't!'

My voice came out strangled, but at least it came. 'You—you really do love Paul, don't you? I thought——'

'That I didn't?' Venetia shook her head. 'I got so I was afraid of showing my real feelings. But I've always been crazy about him, Annabel. I thought, once, that I was in love with Ran, but he knew we weren't right for each other. And Ran being Ran, instead of giving me a polite brush-off he introduced me to his best friend!'

I had never felt so ashamed of myself in my whole life. Hadn't every instinct I possessed told me that Ran wasn't the sort of man who would ever contemplate an affair with somebody else's wife? But instead of listening to my heart I'd allowed myself to misinterpret his words and actions . . . jump to the wrong conclusions. Never mind that Kit had partially influenced my thinking. I should still have known better.

I wished—oh, I wished so much—that I could put the clock back. Back to the afternoon Ran had comforted me in the garden or even further back, to Delos. But I couldn't. Yesterday was yesterday and today was today. Somehow I had to learn to live with the knowledge that I could never ask for explanations nor volunteer any of my own. The mess I had made of things was my own fault—I had no one but myself to blame.

For the first time I was glad of Ran's formal, remote air that kept me at arm's length. We all spent a lot of time at the hospital with Tamsin, and I only ever had close contact with him if I happened to be a passenger in the car he was driving. Even then there was very little communication between us. I would sit and watch the scenery as it flashed past— the silver shimmer of olives, the tall cypresses stabbing the sky like accusing fingers—and I would think how soon all of this would become just a bitter-sweet memory.

My dream holiday was nearly over and though once I would have counted the hours left to me like silver beads on a rosary, now I sometimes felt as though I just couldn't wait to get home to Mother. I had one last lovely day with a radiant Tamsin when she was discharged from hospital and then Ran and Melita and I went to the airport to wave goodbye to her and Paul and Venetia as they set off for Morocco. Paul's arm was around Venetia, tenderly, protectively, and in spite of myself I felt a lump in my throat. His great love for Venetia was tinged with anxiety for her well-being, but I felt sure that his fears were groundless. Now that she was no longer worried and afraid she looked wonderfully well, and the doctor Paul had insisted upon her seeing in Heraklion had assured her that there was no reason why she should not be able to look forward to a carefree pregnancy and an easy birth.

'Isn't it odd to think of someone like Venetia being so pleased about having a baby?' Melita said to me that evening. 'She's not even going to employ anyone to look after it—she's going to look after it herself!' She looked pensive. 'I don't think Kit and I will have babies for a long, long time—perhaps never. They are red and noisy and take up a great deal of one's attention!'

I laughed. 'You're not much more than a baby yourself, Melita. I expect you'll feel quite differently in a few years' time.'

'Oh, you! You're nearly as bad as Venetia! You'll probably have dozens of children when you get married, Annabel—you really like them, don't you?'

I didn't answer and suddenly I saw Melita's face change.

'Oh, Annabel, I'm sorry——'

'Sorry for what?'

Tears sparkled on Melita's long lashes. 'You're the only one—not happy——'

'Rubbish! Of course I am!'

'You're not. I wish—oh, I do wish—you and Ran . . .'

I felt my face flame. 'You're talking nonsense, Melita. Wasting time, too. Now since Kit is taking you out to dinner and you've only got twenty minutes or so to get ready——'

'I wish you'd come, too,' Melita said wistfully. 'You'll be all on your own, since Ran says he's going to spend the evening with Spiros and Annika Stephanos.'

'You don't have to worry about me. I'm going to start packing.' I didn't feel it necessary to inform Melita that if there had been any likelihood of my dining alone with Ran I would have joined her and Kit without the slightest hesitation.

I heard Melita sigh, then she turned away and began fiddling with the things on my dressing table. Checking the irritable protest that rose to my lips, I knelt on the floor to pull my suitcase out from under my bed. I thought, as I started to put in heavy objects like books and shoes, that in some ways it didn't seem nearly four weeks since I'd done this process in reverse, in others it was eternity.

I didn't go downstairs to wave goodbye to Kit and Melita when some half an hour or so later they left for their dinner date but leant out of the window. Melita saw me and waved back, but there was such a curious expression on her face—almost guilty—that I hoped she wasn't going to spend the entire evening worrying in case I was lonely.

I returned to my packing, then realised with a faint prick of annoyance that I'd left several of my books downstairs in the *salotto*. For a moment I hesitated, then decided to fetch them.

Ran was the only person in the *salotto*. He was standing by the window, turning something over and over in his hands. He looked up and saw me hovering in the doorway and his dark brows drew together in a frown. Then he said, 'It's quite safe to come in, you know, Annabel. I'm not going to bite your head off.'

'I left some books over there, on the table. I want to pack them——' I began breathlessly, and then stopped as suddenly I recognised what he was holding in his hands. My silver locket!

A shock of horror went through me. My self-possession deserting me, I started forward.

'My locket! Ran, you've got my locket! You—you—where did you find it? It was on my dressing table——'

'Melita pushed it into my hands just as she was leaving.' There was a strange note in Ran's voice. 'She told me to forget any scruples I might have and to look inside. I haven't, yet, but——'

I was trembling as I realised the extent of Melita's perfidy. 'She had no right to touch it! Ran, please give it back to me!'

Ran's eyes probed my face. 'Annabel, you're trembling. Why is this locket so important to you? Why don't you want me to look inside it?'

I set my teeth. 'Because it happens to be my property, that's why! Ran, give it to me, please! I want it! You're not being fair——'

I tried to snatch at the locket as I spoke, but Ran was too quick for me.

'I agree I'm not being fair, Annabel, but I'm curious to find out just what you're getting in such a state about,' he said softly, and pressed the catch. The locket flew open and I saw his face change as he recognised the photograph inside.

It seemed an age before he spoke. '*My* photograph? Annabel . . . why?'

There was an odd, thick quality in his voice which brought my despair and frustration to a head.

'Because I'm a romantic, that's why,' I said bitterly. 'Oh, Ran, you think you're so clever, don't you, with all those letters after your name, but you weren't ever clever enough to guess that I've been in love with you since I was about twelve years old! Go on—laugh if you want to. I—I don't care any more——'

'*Laugh?*' said Ran. '*Laugh?*' He looked at me incredulously and I felt my bones turn to water as I saw the sudden blaze in his eyes. He took a step forward—then another—and all at once I was in his arms, crushed against him so I could hardly breathe.

'Oh, Annabel, you goose!' he said unsteadily.
'Don't you know even now how I feel about you? Don't you know that I fell in love with you the day I met you in the rose garden and you told me you were looking for Kit? Suddenly I knew you were the only girl I'd ever want to marry, but I didn't think it was any good. I felt sure you'd only ever have room in your heart for Kit, but all the same I made up my mind to invite you to Greece——'

Happiness was breaking over me like a wave as he pressed his cheek against mine.

'But you invited Kit as well——'

'Because I didn't want to take an unfair advantage of you—or him. I knew you'd be vulnerable, Annabel, and I didn't want a holiday romance, I wanted something real and lasting. That's why I was so angry with myself when I made love to you on Delos——'

'Oh, Ran! I thought—I thought——'

'I don't know what *you* thought, but *I* thought I'd messed everything up! You were so cold and unfriendly afterwards, Annabel. Then Kit turned up and I was furious with him because he seemed to be making you desperately unhappy. I really thought you were eating your heart out for him. Then I found you crying in the garden and I believed—I really believed that you'd begun to care for me a little until you told me that whopper about you and Kit. Annabel, *why*? Why did you lie to me? Was it only because of your loyalty to Kit?'

I shook my head. 'No. Ran, I'm sorry. I—I don't know how to say this, but I thought you were still in love with Venetia,' I confessed shamefacedly. 'She's so beautiful—and she seemed so fond of you, and you of her——'

'Well, I'll be damned!' Ran stared at me half in perplexity, half in amusement. 'Listen to me, Annabel. Venetia has never, ever, been anything to me but a very good friend. I've never been in love with her. My heart was an unstormed citadel until just a few weeks ago——'

A little smile curved my lips as I thought how surprised everyone at home would be when they learned that I had become engaged to the 'wrong' Armitage brother.

'My Scorpion,' I whispered lovingly as I drew his head down to mine, and Ran laughed softly, a light growing in his eyes.

'A Scorpion who has far better things to do than sting,' he said, and proceeded to prove it in a way which taught me that, with Ran, I'd always be able to tread a pathway to the stars.

Harlequin Presents...

The beauty of true romance...

The excitement of world travel...

The splendor of first love...

unique love stories for today's woman

Harlequin Presents...
novels of honest,
twentieth-century love,
with characters who
are interesting, vibrant
and alive.

The elegance of love...
The warmth of romance...
The lure of faraway places...

Six new novels, every
month — wherever
paperbacks are sold.

**Make the most of 1980 with your
HARLEQUIN ROMANCE HOROSCOPE and
1980 HARLEQUIN CALENDAR.**

HARLEQUIN READER SERVICE

In U.S.A.
M.P.O. Box 707
Niagara Falls, NY 14302

In Canada
649 Ontario Street
Stratford, Ontario, N5A 6W2

HARLEQUIN SALUTES 1980

Please send me the calendar HARLEQUIN SALUTES 1980. I am
enclosing a check or money order of $3.95 for each calendar ordered,
plus 50¢ to cover postage and handling.

Number of calendars ordered	@ $3.95 each	$_____
N.Y. and N.J. residents add appropriate sales tax		$_____
Postage and handling		$____.50
	TOTAL:	$_____

HARLEQUIN ROMANCE HOROSCOPE

Please send me the following Harlequin Romance Horoscope
volumes. I am enclosing a check or money order of $1.75 for each
volume ordered, plus 40¢ to cover postage and handling.

☐ **Aries**
(Mar. 21-Apr. 20)
☐ **Taurus**
(Apr. 21-May 22)
☐ **Gemini**
(May 23-June 21)
☐ **Cancer**
(June 22-July 22)

☐ **Leo**
(July 23-Aug. 22)
☐ **Virgo**
(Aug. 23-Sept. 22)
☐ **Libra**
(Sept. 23-Oct. 22)
☐ **Scorpio**
(Oct. 23-Nov. 21)

☐ **Sagittarius**
(Nov. 22-Dec. 22)
☐ **Capricorn**
(Dec. 23-Jan. 20)
☐ **Aquarius**
(Jan. 21-Feb. 19)
☐ **Pisces**
(Feb. 20-Mar 20)

Number of volumes checked @ $1.75 each	$_____
N.Y. and N.J. residents add appropriate sales tax	$_____
Postage and handling	$____.40
TOTAL:	$_____
I am enclosing a grand total of	$_____

NAME_____

ADDRESS_____

STATE/PROV._____ ZIP/POSTAL CODE_____

ROM 2294